I0684505

According to Plan
By Sue Barr

Original publication July 2011. Edits and updates have been applied February 2017.

This is a work of fiction. The situations, characters, names and places are products of the author's imagination, or are used factiously. Any resemblance to locales, events, actual persons (living or dead) is entirely coincidental.

Publisher: Sue Barr

Print ISBN: 9780994771827

Cover Design by Rae Monet and Karen Duvall

Text copyright © Susan L. Barr

Sue Barr

To my husband, Rob
I will love you always, even when you won't share your
carrot cake

Sue Barr

Other Books by Sue Barr

WELCOME TO RAVENWOOD

Man of Her Dreams – Book One

Fiancé for Hire – Holiday Novella

PRIDE & PREJUDICE CONTINUED…

Caroline – Book One

Sue Barr

According to Plan

Shelby Stewart's been hired to find socialite, Harrison Grant.

To complicate matters her estranged husband, Jake Steele (aka Tank), shows up looking for Harrison as well, albeit for a very different reason. Harry is the prime suspect in the grisly murder of a call girl in L.A.

Frustration becomes Shelby's newest partner as she attempts to out maneuver her distracting husband in their parallel quest. Tank, on the other hand, is always one step ahead of the game—and is not what or who Shelby thought.

Their adventure escalates from an attempted kidnapping to an explosion with deadly consequences. This is not your average missing person case.

Sue Barr

Chapter One

A hint of rain lingered in the air without breaking the stifling heat. Seated in my office, which I'm sure was a broom closet in a former life, I felt sweat trickle down the inside of my bra. I hated being cooped up on days like this. At least if I was on the job, I could duck into a coffee shop for some air conditioned relief, but I had long overdue paperwork to clear up.

The phone rang and I pounced, hoping it would be something that would set me free.

"Stewart Agencies. This is Shelby."

"Our son is missing."

My heart rate doubled and I grabbed a note pad. "How old is your son, Mr...?

"Grant. Raymond Grant. Harrison is thirty."

I admit to being stunned by the identity of the caller. Raymond Grant was one of our state's more influential political insider, a behind the scenes kind of guy. It was rumored he even had the ear of the President. Harrison, a spoiled chubby little cherub, was his only son. How could he be missing? My take on Harrison was that he wouldn't stray far from the family home, or more specifically, the family money. Still....

"How long has he been missing?"

"I don't have time for small talk, Miss Stewart. Be at

our home in forty-five minutes."

Before I could reply I heard the distinctive click of a phone receiver being hung up and I flopped back into my chair.

Now why would the cream of society call my fledgling company? I'd only been in the Private Investigation business for about a year. As my reputation grew, so had my list of satisfied clients, but I was still the new kid on the block and this didn't make sense.

With a slight shrug, I decided to take it at face value and not be so cynical. Who knows, this job could launch me into a whole new stratosphere – and get me out of the office.

I looked around the brown-paneled room which was my slice of commercial heaven, squeezed between a laundromat and a nail salon. To describe the area as long and narrow would have been generous. Bowling lanes had more space. With the extra money from a high profile job like this, I could buy new carpet and spruce the place up. The curling linoleum, dotted with dubious stains, would not be missed.

A tinkle from the old fashioned bell hung over the front door and the scent of fresh perfume, broke me out of my thoughts. Polly, my best friend and also my secretary, had finally returned from lunch.

"Yo, Pol," I called out and pushed away from the desk to meet her. "You'll never guess who phoned."

She settled at her desk and turned on the computer. "Prince Charming, he's finally leaving what's-her-name and needs you to help rule his magical kingdom."

"All princes are charming, they're just not sincere. Would you believe Raymond Grant?" I waited for her reaction. Polly's family rubbed shoulders with folks like the Grants, not me. Her daddy was into oil. Lots and lots of oil. I'm sure he still wondered why his princess insisted on hanging out with a slum kid like me.

"Wrong number?" Polly asked.

"Aren't you the comedian? Nope, it seems Harrison is missing and the old man hired us to find him."

"Really." Polly grabbed the stack of mail and began sorting it. "I wonder why."

"I don't know." I said. "Maybe they want someone local. You know, keep it off the front page of gossip magazines. I'll find out soon enough, I'm going there right now."

"Okay. Don't forget, movie and pizza tonight, my place."

"You got it."

Headed for the door I stopped mid-step, my mouth instantly dry. Reflected in window of the bakery across the street, was the image of a large man on a motorcycle. I'd recognize that physique anywhere, Jake Steele, aka Tank, aka soon-to-be ex-husband. My heart began pounding and my vision blurred for a brief moment. From excitement or fear, I wasn't sure.

Why couldn't it be anger that had my blood pumping a thousand miles a minute?

"Where are you going?" Polly asked when I swiveled toward the rear of the building.

"Cover for me," I yelled over my shoulder. "Tell him I'm out."

With luck I'd escape through the back door before he saw me. I sidestepped the photocopier and practically flew down the narrow hallway. For one millisecond a twinge of guilt skittered through me, but I quashed it with a vengeance.

Tank and I set a few record with our courtship, marriage and separation. We met at a party, got married three months later and then one year and four months after honeymoon, I returned home from staking out a divorce case and he met me on the front porch with a packed duffel bag. Not once did I believe his big explanation that he had to think over some things. He'd walked away from me, our home and our life. I didn't have to be hit over the head to know he didn't love me. At least not the way I loved him.

I blew out the rear door and had gone almost three steps when strong arms grabbed and twirled me around. I kicked and wriggled until he put me down. About to have an adult conversation – oh heck, I was going to yell at him, he bent down and rocked his lips over mine. Anything I might have said, or thought melted along with the liquid fire spreading through my limbs. I ached to melt into his familiar embrace until my brain finally kicked into gear and I pushed against his chest. I may as well have shoved a brick wall.

"Get off me."

"Is that any way to say hello to your husband?" With one arm around my waist, he dipped his head and attempted to steal another kiss.

I executed a quick side step taught to me by my dad and twisted out of his arms and his lips met nothing but air. I took a small step back and ignored the rapid tattoo of my heart. Tank had a way of making me forget things, like breathing.

"What are you doing here?" I said, ignoring the husband reference, and spared him a glance.

Well over six feet, he had the physique of an oil rigger, built rock hard around pure muscle and adrenalin. A day's growth of stubble darkened his jaw and hair the color of burnished oak brushed his shoulders. Although mirrored glasses hid his eyes, I knew one was green, the other blue, and they missed nothing.

"I was in the area and thought I'd come see y'all." His

rich voice poured over me like melted chocolate. He had a southern drawl and when he talked all slow and sweet, I could listen to him all day. When I was stupid in love, he could have read cereal boxes to me and I wouldn't have cared. My breath hitched at the memories and his knowing smile indicated he'd seen that too.

Time to get off Memory Lane, I had a job to do.

"My office." Without so much as a backward glance, I pivoted and started walking back to the front of the building. He turned and paced his longer stride to match mine. His arm brushed mine and awareness crackled like tiny jolts of electricity along my skin.

The bell above the door jangled as we entered through the front door. Polly, all perky now that Tank was here, sat behind her computer with a wide smile. I glared at her and mouthed, *'You're fired'* as we entered my office, but she ignored my dark look and batted her eyes.

"You've got five minutes," I said as I moved around my desk and sat down.

The image I wished to portray was confident and mildly condescending. The plan was to hear him out, wish him well, send him on his way. One, two, three. No problem.

He pushed some papers out of the way and hitched his hip on the edge of the desk. "I got this lead on one of my cases and it brought me into your neck of the woods. Ever hear of the Grant family?"

Coincidence?

Not in my line of work.

All my senses were on alert. Tank still did PI work, but his client list read like a who's who from Forbes Magazine. What were the odds that the Grant's hired me to find their son, *and* not even five minutes later, Tank shows up, asking about them? I'd hazard a guess and say about a million to one. This may not be the quiet little missing person case Mr. Grant wanted me to believe. Until I figured out what was up and how Tank fit into all this, I'd play dumb.

"I have. They pretty much own the whole town, maybe the whole state."

I watched his face and body language for any tells. Would his eye twitch if he was lying through his teeth? Would he fidget, like I did? Nope. Calm and cool as usual, his smile all laid back like he didn't have a care in the world. That smile lied and I'd like to know why.

"I need your feminine intuition to ride shotgun with me, feel old lady Grant out. Something doesn't feel right and I'm itching in my don't-wanna-itch-place."

Tank had a sixth sense when it came to his work, so I was none too pleased to hear he'd be sniffing around my case.

"What's the tie-in?"

"I'm freelancing for a detective buddy of mine, LAPD. They had a pretty grisly murder of a call girl, lower east side. Word on the street is she had a new john called Harry. Bought her nice clothes, jewelry, all the fixings. I've narrowed the suspect list down to our socialite, Harrison Grant. Thought I'd go rev his motor for a while, see what I could shake loose. Wanna come along for the ride?"

Two things became crystal clear. Tank had to be side-tracked and I needed to talk to the Grant's before he did. One word from Tank and they'd clam up about finding Harrison.

Now I knew why they wanted a small-timer like me. I wouldn't raise any suspicions while I poked around. They obviously hadn't counted on my big bad ex showing up on the same case. If I didn't want to lose the retainer, I had to get there first.

"Where do you plan on staying?" I only asked as a stall

tactic. His answer was not the one I wanted to hear.

"Our house," he shifted closer and I stopped breathing. All I could think of was his stubble darkened chin, his oh-so-kissable mouth, his windblown hair, his…his…everything.

My brain went into a frozen loop. No, no, no, no…

"No." I finally pushed the word through stiff lips.

"Considering I hold the deed, this is a moot point."

"We're not married—"

"Oh, yes we are." He stopped any further words coming out of my mouth with one warning look.

"You could have fooled me," I muttered in defiance.

For the zillionth time, I wondered what the statute of limitations was on stupid decisions. Marrying him had to top the list.

He pushed off the desk and moved around to stand in front of me. Too late, I realized my error. By sitting behind the desk, I'd boxed myself in. That Tank was aware of this became evident by the smile tugging at the corner of his lips. He drew close enough that I caught his scent.

Peppermint!

I stifled a deep groan. I used to love peppermint.

Minty breath brushed my temple and I clutched the arms of the chair in a death grip. No matter what he said, or did, I'd stay in control.

"You will always be my wife. Til death do us part, sweetheart." Warm lips covered mine.

My eyes flew open when he broke off the kiss. With his face mere inches from mine, I noted his eyes darken with desire. So, he wasn't unaffected either. The girlfriend must be holding out on him and he needed another type of itch scratched. Hah! Good luck, it wouldn't be me, that's for darn sure.

"We'll talk later. I'm going to drop off my gear." He

straightened and walked out of my office with a lethal grace, looking like he kissed girls senseless all the time. Still a tad bemused from the kiss, I watched him leave. His jeans, low on his hips, the material faded and worn, caressed him like an old friend. I loved the way he filled out those jeans. Oh Nantucket! I forgot to tell him *where* he could stay. Why did my noodle go on vacation whenever he was around?

"Guest bedroom only," I called after him. "Tank?"

The front door slammed. A heartfelt sigh came from the next room. Most likely my newly fired secretary, drooling over Tank again.

"Pull it back in, Polly. I can hear dripping from here."

"Oh my, he's the most gorgeous man ever," she sighed out in a breathy whoosh. I knew she'd have her chin propped in the palm of her hand, all gooey and dreamy eyed, watching Tank through the front window. "Honey, I don't know why you won't take him back. If he was mine, I'd be in his front pocket all day."

"Well, you can have him. Those days are over for me." I grabbed my purse and the keys to my car. "See you tonight." I should have about an hour head start. By the time he reached my place, dropped his stuff off and drove out to the Grant's, I'd be long gone.

I loved it when a plan worked.

*****

Tank swung his leg over the motorcycle, slid the sunglasses on and looked toward Shelby's office. A touch of pride swelled his heart for a brief moment. She'd done pretty well and he knew it'd been rough. First, she'd had to get past the hurt of him leaving and then continue the fledgling business they'd started.

He didn't regret leaving her, even though it was the

toughest thing he'd ever done in his entire life. When he saw the confused hurt in her eyes the night he'd walked out, he almost turned back, but with her life in danger he had to go.

That was the risk you took when you worked undercover and a slime ball member of a mafia run business got spooked. Carlos began nosing around, asking a lot of questions and it would have been only a matter of time before he found out about Shelby. To keep her safe, Tank made everyone think they'd split. Not a perfect plan, but one that worked.

And worked too well, she believed he left her for another woman.

Then last week, Carlos had permanently retired, without a pension. He wouldn't need it at Mount Pleasant Cemetery. After Tank wrapped up this case with Harrison, he planned on telling Shelby why he left. Nothing would stop him from breaking down walls to recapture the trust of the only woman who made his knees buckle.

He started the bike and rumbled down the street. When he was sure he was out of Polly's sight, he backed into an alley with a clear view of Shelby's office and car, and waited.

Shelby was as beautiful today as the first time he met her. Clear blue eyes and blonde curls that fell to her waist when it wasn't bunched into a messy top knot, like today. And he knew that although petite, she'd lay you out faster than you could blink. Her father had been a cop, a good one, and before he died, he made sure his little girl could take care of herself.

The cough and sputter of a familiar engine caught his attention. Hearing the death bucket she drove brought a smile to his lips. He knew she could afford a better car, but she clung tenaciously to her beat-up baby. The Blue Bomb, as she lovingly called it. Shelby inherited it and the payments when her mother died.

Keeping a few cars between them, he followed the Blue Bomb through town, dropping back a bit further when she hit the outskirts and then stopped completely once he knew for sure where she was going. She was headed for Cedar Heights, where Raymond and Estelle Grant lived.

He figured he had time for a coffee and pie, so he executed a lazy U-turn and went back to a little diner tucked by the side of the road. From there he had a clear view of the highway and if she left before he was done, he'd see her go by in a haze of blue smoke.

He'd just been served a piece of home-made pecan pie and coffee when his phone vibrated in his pocket. Caller ID showed it was the cell phone Raymond Grant received by courier that morning along with explicit instructions. With a dark smile, Tank answered, "Steele."

"I got your message, Agent Steele." Raymond's voice betrayed tension. It sizzled through the phone. "Now what?"

"She'll be there soon."

"She better not get in the way. If anything happens to Harrison—"

"Nothing will happen to Harry." Tank interrupted. "Stick with what we agreed upon, nothing more."

There was a pause at the other end and then Raymond came back on the phone. "She's here. I've got to go. Estelle is very upset with all of this. Are you sure this Stewart girl can do the job?"

Tank grinned. Shelby was thorough and would follow every lead on Harrison. He'd been amazed at how quickly she'd adapted to being a P.I. when they started their business. The detective gene must run in the family. "Oh yeah, she's absolutely right for this job. I'll be in touch."

He ended the call and emptied three sugar packets into his coffee. He wished he could be a fly on the wall. It'd be fun to see how Shelby handled Estelle Grant.

If the Grant's landlines had been tapped, as he suspected, then Shelby's firm being hired would cement the belief Harrison had gone A.W.O.L. Shelby didn't need to know Harry was in protective custody, turning state's evidence against a major piece of dirt referred to as 'The Big Boss.' To keep Harry's involvement with Tank's agency under wraps, it was vital she asked questions around town, supporting the story that Harrison was missing.

When Tank thought enough time had passed, he paid his bill, re-mounted his bike and drove to the entrance of the Grant's driveway. After parking, he kicked out the stand, leaned back on the seat and got comfortable. Shelby had some explaining to do.

This could be a whole lot of fun.

Sue Barr

Chapter Two

I crunched up the long drive which led to the Grant's estate and parked in front of an enormous mansion, straight out of *Gone With the Wind*. The façade, complete with pillars and a wraparound porch only required a southern belle in a large, frilly hoop dress to come waltzing around the corner.

Expecting a butler, someone like Lurch from the *Addams Family*, my line of sight was raised when the door swung open. Slowly I brought my gaze down to the smallest, meanest looking woman I had ever seen. A smidge over five feet, she was almost as wide as she was tall. With one glance she summed me up and her lip curled into a sneer. I guess I came up short.

I choked back a snort at my own pun and the little gnome must have caught it.

"We don't want none," she barked and tried slamming the door in my face.

I put my boot out to stop the door from closing, flipped open my wallet and extracted one of my brand new business cards. "Stewart Investigations," I said, handing it to her. "Mr. Grant's expecting me."

She screwed her face into a scowl and stared at my card. Satisfied, she grudgingly opened the door. "You stay put. I'll tell the mister you're here." She moved away with amazing speed and I stepped further inside and stopped.

If I were in a cartoon, I'd have been portrayed with my lower jaw hitting the floor in a big wet splat.

Polished marble floors gleamed in the foyer. A chandelier, which had to weigh a thousand pounds, hung over a mahogany table that would have comfortably sat a family of twelve. The entrance, dominated by a central staircase, caught my imagination and I could almost see the ghost of Rhett Butler, looking up at Miss Scarlett. I was now convinced whoever built this house loved *Gone With the Wind* as much as me.

Within minutes the housekeeper returned and asked me to follow her. She ushered me toward a room just off the entranceway.

"Thank you, Hannah." A soft, Georgia peach voice lilted toward us. Ah, there she was, the reincarnated Scarlett O'Hara. "You can bring in the lemonade and cake now."

The voice belonged to society's darling, Estelle Grant.

"Yes, Mrs. Grant, right away." The surly servant disappeared beneath a thin veneer of civility.

I stepped into a stylish room, dotted with several couches and chairs placed to draw people's eye toward an elegant fireplace. In the middle of this *Better Homes & Garden* vignette sat Estelle. She looked like a porcelain doll—fragile, pink, and fluffy. In her hand she clutched a lace hanky. I was a little disappointed. I'd expected a vision in red, with rich dark curls and an elegantly raised eye brow.

"Mrs. Grant? I'm Shelby Stewart. Your husband called earlier."

I strode forward and held out my hand. With a slight hesitation she placed her frail one in mine. After a brief touch of our fingers, she withdrew and tucked her hand beneath the hanky. Although the movement was slight, I'd bet money she wiped her fingers off. Without asking, I sat on the chair opposite her, and Estelle's lips pursed ever so slightly. I guess I should have waited for the royal nod or something.

"Thank you for coming so soon." Estelle said. "This is such a trying time for our family."

"Is Mr. Grant here?"

"Raymond?" She paused, her eyes shifting to the door at the far side of the room. "He's making a phone call. He'll be with us shortly."

A rattling noise announced the return of Hannah. Mrs. Grant looked toward the door, relief evident on her pinched face. "Set it over there Hannah," indicating the glass coffee table in front of us.

Hannah carried a silver tray, loaded down with cakes, cookies and a pitcher of lemonade. Under the watchful eye of Mrs. Grant she poured us each a glass. After placing the jug on the tray, she turned to leave.

"Hannah?"

"Yes, Mrs. Grant?"

"Make sure Bobbi-Jo cleans that little mess I spotted by the gazebo this morning."

"Yes, Mrs. Grant." Hannah clumped out of the room.

Estelle offered me a cookie, which I declined. As she set the plate on the table she explained, "We had the gazebo re-stained and our dog Chester keeps getting into the plants. The dirt he digs flies up and sticks to the walls."

After taking a sip of her tea she fell into silence. I attempted to engage her in small talk, anything beyond the weather, but she either had nothing to say, or had the personality of a dish rag. I leaned strongly in favor of the dish rag. Ten minutes I'd never get back passed before Mr. Grant joined us.

A tall, striking man, he stepped into the room. His whole demeanor portrayed a tense nervousness. No smile crossed his lips, but that would be expected since Harrison was their only child.

"I'm sorry I kept you waiting. Thank you for coming so quickly." He sat next to his wife.

"Shall we get started?" I asked, looking at both of them on the sofa. Mr. Grant nodded. Not wanting to waste any more time I pulled a simple notebook and pen from my purse and flipped open to a clean page.

"When did you last hear from Harrison? Does he call home often?"

I wanted a sense of their relationship, anything which might give a clue to Harrison's mind-set.

"Harrison's been living in Los Angeles for over a year now. Although he juggles a very hectic business and social calendar he calls home every Sunday..." Mrs. Grant brought the hanky to her nose. She stifled a small hiccupping sob and turned into Mr. Grant's shoulder. With a few pats and a squeeze on her arm, she quieted.

And the Award goes to....

I had to bite the inside of my cheek to keep from smiling. When had I become such a cynic? Probably right about the time Tank walked out and broke my heart. The sobs could be genuine, but that tiny voice inside my head coldly pointed out how not one single tear escaped her carefully made up eyes.

"He hasn't called for over three weeks." Mr. Edwards bit out, "Not one single phone call, e-mail, nothing."

I noted Mr. Grant was angered by Harrison's disappearance. Most families were frantic with worry, not annoyed. Had Harrison done this sort of thing before? That would explain the tension which permeated the room.

Yet, something about Mrs. Grant didn't ring true. While we waited for her husband, she hadn't talked about Harrison. Not even once. In my line of work you looked for nonverbal clues, like body language. Estelle Grant worried more about her gazebo than her only child and sipped lemonade. An underlying current of nervousness lay like a film across their skin, evident by the tic in Mr. Grant's jaw.

I began scribbling in my notepad. The Grants would think I believed them, but in reality, I'd started a grocery list. Milk, cheese, rib-eye steaks, chocolate buds. I scratched the steaks off. They were Tank's favorite and I would NOT buy food for him.

A curious thought struck me at the reminder of Tank. Could their unease stem from the fact they knew Harrison was implicated in the murder of a hooker? I decided to broach the subject in a round-about way.

"Has Harrison met anyone? Someone he may have gone away with?"

I watched Mr. Grant's reaction closely.

"He met a girl, Lulu." He spat out her name, venom tingeing his voice. "Don't know much about her, except he seems mighty enamored with her. His credit card bills are staggering."

Interesting... Harrison didn't foot his own bills. I added bread to the list.

Mr. Grant stood and stalked over to the window, shoving clenched hands into his trouser pockets while he stared out over his expansive grounds. His stance remained rigid. I'd have bet Polly's trust fund he knew of Harrison's possible involvement with Lulu's murder. It looked like he had no intention of sharing this information with me.

Fair trade, I didn't plan on telling him I knew Harrison was a suspect in a murder investigation, or that Lulu was a hooker. I could play dumb blonde all day if that's what he wanted. Mrs. Grant took a tiny sip of her lemonade, keeping her face averted.

An uncomfortable pause stretched between us.

I looked down at my sparse notes above the grocery list. There was nothing here for me to go on. "What makes you think Harrison is missing and didn't just take off? Was he having problems at work?"

Mr. Grant turned from the window, his voice betraying anger. "My son would never just *take off*. He loves his mother more than life—" Estelle sobbed. "Someone stopped him from contacting us."

The *'someone'* caught my ear, so I made yet another note. Shampoo. An imp of mischief prompted the next question. "Have you called the police in Los Angeles? The authorities have been alerted he's missing, right?"

I hit the jackpot with that question. Mr. Grant's face turned a mottled shade of purple and Mrs. Grant's knuckles went snow white clutching a now shredded hanky. *I wonder if she'll swoon.* It was time to let them off the hook. Without words they'd spoken volumes already.

"Well... I'm sure you've called them. You can always send me the name of his case investigator if you think I need it."

I closed the notebook, shoving both it and the pen back into my purse. "I can't think of anything more right now. Would you mind if I checked out Harrison's condo? I'd like to get a feel for his style. Maybe he left something behind that will help."

Mr. Grant walked over to a small escritoire and retrieved something out of the drawer. He wrote down information on a slip of paper, then came over and handed it to me along with a key.

"Here. This is Harrison's condo key and address."

****

I headed down the long driveway mulling over my strange, short visit with the Grants and came to a screeching halt when I saw Tank stretched out on his motorbike. He looked big, bad, and dangerous.

Uncertain how to proceed I chewed my lip. I could ask him to move. I snorted in disdain. Tank didn't do anything but what he wanted. Me asking nicely wouldn't make him budge an inch. I could always drive around, but that would tear up the manicured lawn and mow down a few well-placed shrubs.

The sobering thought of the Grant's calling the cops forced me to deal with him in an adult manner. Last thing I needed was one of my dad's old buddies showing up and catching us in the middle of a domestic quarrel. With that in mind I climbed out of the car and walked to where Tank reclined, looking far too casual for my taste. Stopping just a shade out of his reach, I hooked my thumbs in my front jean pockets and watched him watch me.

He lifted his mirrored sunglasses and slid them onto his head. "Looks like we got us a conflict."

"How'd you know I was here?"

I stepped back when he leaned forward, resting an oh-so-muscular arm on his knee.

"Darlin', when you said I could stay at the house without a fight, I knew something's up. You never go sweet on me, so I followed. Mind telling me what's going on?"

"Nope."

"Come on. I scratch your back, you scratch mine. Kinda like the old days.?"

Bitter-sweet memories washed over me and I closed my

eyes as pain carved yet another tiny piece from my heart. The *'old days'* when we could almost read each other's thoughts we'd been so in tune. But I hadn't been as intuitive as I thought or I'd have known he'd tired of me long before he left.

I re-opened my eyes and looked directly into his. "Wrong question to ask the ex-wife, Tank. You're losing your touch. I'm going home." For a brief moment I thought remorse flickered in those sharp, see everything eyes, but that was most likely wishful thinking on my part. "The offer of the guest room is rescinded. Get a motel."

"Nice try." He slid his glasses back on and started the bike. "I'll mosey on up to the Grant's, and take a look around. Maybe have a good long talk with Harry if he's there. See you later."

I watched as he throttled his bike and roared up the manicured drive. I'd love to watch the hobbit housekeeper take him on but I had errands to run and then go home to pack for my trip to L.A.

Chapter Three

Harrison was missing, yet his parents didn't act worried. What was it that didn't ring true? And why didn't they call off the search after Tank showed up? Something was off and danced around the edges of my brain, going in circles. Arrangements needed to be made, so I called Polly.

"How'd the meeting go?" she asked.

"Strange is the only word I can think of right now."

My phone teetered on my shoulder as I juggled my purse, the few groceries I'd picked up and car keys. All this, while unlocking the front door. "I need you to book a flight for me to L.A., day after tomorrow. Also, see if you can book me into a hotel near Hollywood Boulevard. I'm going to check out the area, talk to some of Hollywood's leading ladies and want to stay at a hotel close by."

"Leading ladies? Like Jennifer Aniston? " Polly sounded excited.

"I meant hookers. You know. Hookers? Leading ladies?" Nothing but dead air floated through the phone. "Forget it. I'll see you later tonight."

I ended the call and shouldered the door open. Just as I crossed the threshold, my land line rang. I ran to the kitchen, dropped my packages and grabbed the receiver on the fourth ring.

"Hello?"

"Good afternoon, I'm glad I caught you at home."

Why hadn't I looked at the call display? Tension snaked up the back of my neck. He always seemed to know when I was home.

"What do you want, Regis?"

My neighbor, Regis, had the personality of a gnat. He didn't get the nuances of social civility. When he talked, you wished you were elsewhere, anywhere but there. You'd watch grass grow because it was more exciting. Not all of us were interested in the mating habits of Puffins, or whatever held his fancy this month.

"I called because I have made a discovery and wondered if I might stop by your office tomorrow."

I pictured him pushing his glasses up the bridge of his nose. The fine hairs on my arms rose straight up at the thought of Regis cornering me in my office. I'd take Tank over him every day, all day before that happened. Time to nip this baby in the bud.

"I won't have time, my calendar is quite full. Is this all you called about?"

"I'd hoped you would consent to dine with mother and me one evening this week."

I was positive I heard his bowtie spinning and the crack of his mother's whip.

"Regis, we talked about this before. I'm going to say no, *again*. Call Penelope. She's anxious to show you..." *Geez, what did Penny have again?* "Whatever it is she's growing in her garage. You'd have a lot in common."

"Shelby, Mother has—"

I hung up and gave my body a shake, like a kid at school who got cootie germs. Regis phoned me on a regular basis asking me on dates, *with his mother*. He'd latched on to me when we were kids and I could only handle him in small doses. There was a slimy, ick factor about him and it had nothing to do with the three pounds of Brylcreem in his hair.

Putting away groceries, I sighed when I noticed I'd purchased most of Tank's favorite foods. I stared at the can of whipped cream before putting it in the fridge beside the pecan pie. I may have told him to go to a motel, but I knew he'd stay here.

I braced my hands on the counter and lowered my head. Why couldn't I move on? I'd figured it out that he'd left me for another woman. What did she offer that would tempt him from what seemed to be a wonderful, loving marriage? I had no answers and until today, I hadn't spoken with Tank in over three months. I also hadn't been kissed like I was desirable either.

Since Tank left I'd been a virtual hermit, only exiting my cave to work. The thought of another man getting close to me made me want to shrivel up into a ball and wail. So, I had issues with intimacy and it was all *his* fault. I headed upstairs and threw my purse on the bed. Maybe long hot shower would wash my heartache away. A girl could hope.

****

Tank let himself into Shelby's house and heard the shower. There had been a time when he'd have joined her, but all that was gone. His rights as her husband were on hold until she was apprised of the whole situation. Only one other person close to Shelby knew he was a Federal Agent, and she'd sworn on a stack of cream filled donuts she wouldn't give away his secret.

This case with Harrison couldn't end soon enough for him. The slimy little worm wouldn't give them the information needed to close in on Big Boss. He did let slip there was someone else involved. Someone from this town.

Tank knew he was close to closing the case, he could

taste it. Nervous energy thrummed through his veins and if he were superstitious, like his partner Rodi, he'd bet everything on them discovering who Big Boss was.

Thinking of Rodi made him realize his inside man hadn't contacted him in a while. Not unusual when you work deep undercover, but Rodi always tried to leave an encrypted message every two weeks.

Tank paused outside the master bedroom door and surveyed the room before taking a step inside. Nothing had changed much, except anything that belonged to him was hidden or thrown away. A wry grin tipped his lip. Most likely thrown out or burned. Maybe both.

He walked to the dresser and picked up a bottle of her favorite perfume, drawing in the scent. Immediately he was transported back to the first time he met her, at a party on the beach. Across the fire he'd been mesmerized by the woman with hair the color of ripened wheat, cascading down her back in soft curls. And when they'd come face to face, one of the first things he did was kiss her.

Turned out to be a wrong move, but he couldn't help himself. When her gaze met his, he knew right then and there he'd marry her. It took a few months to convince Shelby of that, *after* he'd located her. The little minx gave him the number to a funeral home when he asked for her number.

The shower shut off and he heard the sounds of Shelby moving around the bathroom. He stood by the walk-in closet door and leaned one shoulder against the door jamb. Within minutes she opened the door, looking flushed with her hair twisted up into a clip and a warm, fuzzy housecoat wrapped around her body. She hadn't seen him yet, so he waited until she stopped in front of the dresser and looked into the mirror, catching his reflection.

Her eyes widened and then closed. He pushed away from the door. "Hey, darlin'."

****

My thoughts over the past few hours had been all about Tank, and then I stepped into bedroom and saw him. A sense of déjà vu washed over me and I closed my eyes so he couldn't see my pain.

Tank's hand on my shoulder, turning me to face him, surprised me. I thought he'd step away, but instead he cupped my face, held my gaze and smiled a lazy smile. The one that made me fall in love with him the first time. He slipped a finger under my chin and caressed my cheek with his thumb. I wanted to press into his hand and rub my cheek against his palm. It took everything inside me to remain still.

He lowered his head and took possession of my mouth. Love, hurt, and anger combined and spread out from my heart and through my body. I stood, bathed in all these conflicting emotions and knew I still loved him. He broke the kiss and rested his forehead on mine.

I had to be realistic. He might be here for only a few hours. Could my heart take him leaving again? The cold answer was, no.

"Tank—"

"Shh….." He silenced me with a finger on my lips. "I don't mean to complicate things, but I can't stay away. And God knows I tried." He walked over to my king-sized bed and lay down, making it look like a doll's toy. He stretched out and, long legs crossed at the ankles, linked his hands behind his head and watched me. His biceps tensed and flexed with perfection.

I turned toward the dresser and grabbed a handful of underwear, shoving them into the cavernous pocket of my housecoat before Tank could see them. "You can't waltz into my bedroom—"

"Our bedroom," he corrected.

"—and think we can go on like nothing happened. You made your choice."

I glanced over to the bed where he looked like the poster boy for Tall, Dark and Dangerous. Did he get my meaning? Marital relations were *not* going to happen. Not tonight, not tomorrow, maybe not ever. He'd left me for another woman and my stomach clenched at the thought of him touching her. Loving her. Tasting her—

The taste of bile was bitter in my mouth as I turned toward the dressing room. I'd spent countless nights, crying myself to sleep at the thought of him loving another woman the way he'd loved me. It had taken everything inside me to crawl out of that hole of self-pity and I wasn't going back.

I grabbed the closest tee shirt which said, *'If you don't like what I'm cookin', stay out of the kitchen'* and a pair of jeans. With my skin still being moist from the shower, the jeans wouldn't shimmy up over my hip as far as I'd like, but I couldn't leave Tank alone any longer. I re-entered the bedroom, and stopped cold in the doorway.

My purse lay open and Tank was reading my notes from the Grant family meeting. He held up the open book and raised one eyebrow in question. "Grocery list?"

I stomped over and snatched the notebook out of his hand before grabbing my purse. Everything spilled out, which ratcheted my frustration up another level. I threw the purse back onto the bed.

"Get out!" I hissed, pointing to the door. "You have no right to go through my private papers. And you're staying in the guest room, not here." Clutching the notebook to my chest, I crossed over to the bedroom door and held it open.

"Out!"

He pushed off the bed and strolled out of my bedroom. But not before he paused, lightly touched the exposed skin where my jeans had refused to go further, and leaned in. His warm breath feathered my ear, "Glad to see you still have your tattoo."

Sue Barr

Chapter Four

Ah, yes, the tattoo. On my right hip I had a tattoo of a small 'T' with a stylistic heart wrapped around it. During our wild, crazy honeymoon in Cancun with Tank I'd gotten it to show how much he was in my heart. That promise of love walked out my front door, but the tat was forever. Lucky me.

I wandered into the ensuite bathroom and perched on the edge of the tub. I tried to have a backbone when it came to Tank but he was my Achilles Heel. This was the twenty-first century. Tank could have sex with whomever he wanted and, technically, so could I, except Tank had been my first and only lover and I wouldn't betray the bonds of marriage.

I stood and started blow drying my hair. Staring at my reflection, I gave my 'self' a pep talk.

"You're a strong woman. You don't need Tank to validate who you are. Get the job done and don't let him get under your skin." Firm with resolve to distance myself emotionally from Tank, I wandered down to the kitchen where I found him making coffee. Without turning he said, "That wasn't nice, what you did out at the Grants. You could have warned me about the guard troll."

How quickly I'd forgotten about Hannah. I choked back a little giggle. "What's the matter Tank, couldn't handle a little old lady?"

"Do you still take your coffee black?" He reached into

the cupboard and brought down sugar for his coffee.

Tank continued to move around the kitchen with ease. I longed to reach out and rub his back like I had in the past. To know that with one touch, he'd turn around, gather me into his arms and kiss me senseless. My hand rose, but then dropped back by my side.

This camaraderie in the kitchen brought back a lot of memories I chose to forget. Tears formed and my eyes burned. My firm resolve was melting as fast as the sugar in his coffee.

"What did the Grants want to see you for?" He took my cup and poured coffee into it. Quickly, I dashed the tears away with the back of my hand. I reached around and grabbed the mug.

"Nothing much. They want me to track down a cousin or something. She has to sign some papers for their business."

I hated lying. It went against every Sunday school lesson I'd learned and Pastor Nolan's preaching. Whoever said lying could be cathartic for a bruised psyche was dead wrong. He shook his head, turned around and poured a third spoonful of sugar into his mug.

Coffee in hand, I walked into the living room. I set the mug down and flopped into my easy chair before turning on the television. Tank stayed in the kitchen and set up his lap top at the kitchen table.

It was surreal, having Tank in the next room working while I watched television. We'd fallen right back into the routine we had before he left. I wasn't sure if that was a good thing, or a bad thing. After the local news, I remembered my date with Polly. I placed my cup in the dishwasher, headed for the front door and had just grabbed my purse when a creak echoed down the hall.

Tank stood in the entrance of the kitchen, his large frame filling the doorway. "Where are you going?"

"Polly's," My throat felt tight, "It's our movie night."

"That's right. It's Tuesday." He turned back into the kitchen.

After this case I was getting my head examined. On my own I was a confident, independent woman. Tank showed up and suddenly I became a blubbering, mindless, love-starved moron. There must be workshops I could take that addressed this kind of thing. The gym I went to always had posters advertising self-help classes. I was going to sign up for one and take back control of my life, right after my trip to L.A.

When I got to Polly's my jaw ached from clenching my teeth. Soft light from recessed pot lights pooled onto her front entrance and when she opened the door, I smelled popcorn.

"I wondered when you'd get here, you're late." She wore a fluffy pink robe and bunny slippers, her face free from any make-up. I was probably the only person on earth who ever saw Polly this way. Not her usual, sophisticated style. Most people probably thought she reclined about her mansion in silk robes and sexy slip-on mules.

"I'm sorry, Tank's at my place." I pushed by her and made my way to the theatre room, where she'd set up the DVD.

"Ah. That explains it." Polly shut the door and followed me in. She offered me a cola before sitting and re-wrapping herself in a homemade afghan.

I plopped down on the other end of the sofa and grabbed a bowl of popcorn. Harley, her tea-cup Yorkie, pattered in and jumped up on my lap. "So what are we watching?"

"*Casablanca*."

My shoulders slumped. Not again. It was so...so... black and white. And Humphrey Bogart didn't do it for me as a leading man. Now, if Rick Blaine was played by Henry Cavill, I'd wear the DVD out.

"We've seen it a gazillion times. Isn't there anything else? Something that's been produced in this century? In color? I'll even watch *Steel Magnolias* again."

"Nope, Casablanca. I love when Rick says to Isla, *I remember everything. The Germans wore gray. You wore blue*."

"All right, but you'll be sorry next month. For my choice I'm thinking *Space Ship Troopers... Part II*." It was Polly's turn to groan.

"Oh, shush. You love this movie as much as me. I've seen you cry when she has to leave Rick." She pointed the remote control at the TV and started the movie.

I grabbed another handful of popcorn and settled in, allowing Harley to eat out of my hand while the credits rolled.

"At least Isla left Rick, not the other way around." I whispered to Harley, who panted in agreement, his button eyes sparkling like bright berries.

I forgot how good Polly's hearing was. One of the things that made her a good secretary.

"Hon, you have *got* to stop looking back. Keep doing that and you'll never see the good things ahead of you." She grabbed some popcorn out of my bowl. "Take the bull by the horns. Talk to Tank about why he left. Get it out in the open."

"He didn't leave, I kicked him out." I pulled my bowl away from her.

"That's horse puckey and you know it. This is me you're talking to. He walked out and you fell apart. You need to find out why or every time he comes around, you'll keep spinning your wheels."

"He won't keep coming around. Once this case is wrapped up he'll scamper back to his new girlfriend."

"Are you sure? All I'm saying is, you need to talk. You need to know why he left."

I knew she was right, but I was glad the movie started so she wouldn't see tears trickle down my face. Tears Harley softly licked off my cheek. Even if she had, she wouldn't have commented. Polly never betrayed confidences. Not even when I snuck out with Ben Grady after I'd been grounded.

****

Later that night, as I lay in bed, my mind scampered in a million directions. I had to devise a plan to side track Tank and keep him from discovering I was going to L.A. Ideally he'd leave again – my heart cramped – and I wouldn't have to worry, but I had a feeling he was here for a while. And because he was my roommate-du-jour, he'd figure out pretty fast I was up to something.

Tank had Spidey senses, like Peter Parker's Spiderman, when it came to me, so I needed him deaf and blind. Call it self-preservation or just plain pride, but I didn't want him in my business. He lost that privilege when he moved out.

The next day at work I hatched and discarded idea after idea. Tank knew me too well. It was on the drive home, when I saw an ad for 'Don't Drink and Drive,' the plan hit me. Get him drunk. Then he'd pass out and while he slept like a baby, I'd pack my bags and leave.

All I had to do was figure out how much it would take to knock him out. Tank could put back a few beers, but I'd never seen him drunk and the whole operation had to be subtle or his internal radar would start pinging. I decided to start with something small, like drinks with dinner. That would work. My drink would be sipped and I'd top his up on a regular basis.

After I'd been home for about an hour I heard keys hitting the hall table. There was a time when I'd drop everything, run down the hall and jump into his arms. I continued to grate parmesan.

"Mmm, smells good. What are we having?" Tank came into the kitchen and sat at the island. He placed his laptop bag on the floor beside his stool.

"Lasagna and salad. Want a drink?"

"Nah. I'm good. Can I help?"

He came around and started ripping apart the romaine. Plan A shot down before it even started. On to Plan B—wine with dinner.

Supper was quiet. There were too many emotional landmines we both were dancing around. Also, my thoughts were focused on creating a Plan C. He'd refused the offer of wine with his meal. This was proving more difficult than I imagined.

While I cleared the table, he settled on the couch. Even though we were no longer a couple I admit to being miffed when he brought out his laptop. Soon he was texting, checking messages and generally ignoring me. Fine by me, I had my own stuff to do.

I sat and twirled my hair.

Last night Polly suggested we go shopping and now I wished I hadn't blown her off. She would have helped me think of devious ways to get Tank drunk.

Through my eyelashes, I observed Tank. Totally immersed in his work, his rugged face illuminated by the artificial light from his laptop screen, he had no idea I watched him. Every line, every angle of his face was familiar. I knew if he smiled, one lone dimple would appear. His face would be rough to my touch from the five o-clock shadow dusting the lower half of his face. His breath warm on my palm as he turned to kiss it.

A familiar ache tightened my chest. He was no longer mine and the sooner I solved this case and he waved good-bye, the better.

Reigning in my thoughts, I re-focused on my plan. I chewed my lip and twirled my hair some more. Then it hit me. Why didn't I think of this sooner? Polly had given me some sleeping pills after Tank left and there was almost a full bottle left.

I needed to get him into the hard stuff, so I could mask it. He'd never know I slipped a little something 'extra' into his beverage. And, with any luck, he'd be gone to la la land in no time. Great plan in theory, but how would I get him to drink? He'd refused every offer so far tonight. Mentally I slapped my palm against my forehead. I'd been making the wrong offer.

I would utilize the time-honored method of diversion, a game of strip pool. No way would I play strip poker; Tank would have me naked in two straight hands. But at pool—I could take the guy. We played this a lot and I'd beaten him regularly.

Time to put Plan C in motion.

"Tank, I'm bored." I maneuvered myself so I lay draped over the big easy chair, letting my leg swing back and forth over the arm. "Wanna play strip pool?"

His head rose, like a buck scenting a doe in heat. He's not stupid, he had to know I was up to something, but he was willing to play along. After putting away his laptop, he leaned back and stretched his arms across the back of the couch, all smug and cocky. "Rack 'em up, darlin'. Call me when you're ready to break."

"I'll mix some drinks, you rack and break. I'll be right down."

As always, I loved it when a plan worked.

Chapter Five

The sound of balls being racked floated up the stairs while I prepared the drinks. Tank had gone for it. Tomorrow morning he'd be pretty embarrassed about falling for my ruse. In a small way, I felt bad for him.

How could I even hint at having sexual relations with Tank when we hadn't worked out our problems? Deceit had an insidious way of making a person do unethical things. On the verge of backing down, I mentally pictured him kissing another woman and twisted open the bottle.

I estimated an ounce for each drink and poured the amber liquid over ice cubes, followed by some cola. For extra insurance, and because I was still mad at him, I threw another splash of rum into Tank's glass.

I rummaged through my medicine cabinet, found the sleeping pills Polly gave me and shook out two little blue capsules. They were kind of small and Tank was pretty big, so I added one more. Three should keep him out of the way until I was safely in the air, enjoying my complimentary in-flight package of pretzels. After breaking them open, I poured the powder into his glass and threw the tiny casings in the garbage.

It took only a few seconds to stir the drink before heading downstairs and hand Tank his before placing mine on the bar behind him. I walked over to the wall-mounted rack and grabbed my cue stick. Confidence surged through me as I returned to where he stood, drink in hand. I reached around and picked up mine.

"Here's to me kicking your butt." I tapped my glass against his and watched him take a nice long swallow. I hid a smile against my glass and enjoyed a sip too. It tasted good. Tasted like victory.

"Best two out of three?" I asked.

Tank nodded the affirmative, placed his drink on the bar and walked over to the table. He lined up his shot and with a quick, powerful hit, sank two balls.

Lucky break.

He moved around the table, analyzing all angles and then sank one, two, three balls in a row. Impressed, I sipped my rum. Two of his balls were left on the table when he missed the fourth shot. With a slight shrug, he turned to face me. "Let's see what you got, darlin'."

"Ha. What I *got* is a perfectly executed game about to happen. Stand aside."

I chalked my cue stick while I walked around, checking out the lay of the table. I was pretty good at pool, I had to be. In my line of work, you hung out at bars and pool halls, talking to people and I'd picked up a few tricks. I made some fancy bank shots, double backs, and sank four in a row.

My fifth shot was impossible to execute, so as a nasty treat, I tapped my ball and left the white cue ball tucked behind it. The only way he could make the shot was by hitting the cue ball down the length of the table, strike a precise, exact location and roll back, just kissing his ball so it would slide into the pocket.

Laughing outright I said, "Let's see you get out of this one, big boy." I toasted him with my drink again.

"I've got moves you've never seen, babe." A wolfish

grin crossed his lips.

Normal Tank was dangerous, but playful Tank was lethal and a familiar energy sizzled through my system. He threw back about half his rum, put down the glass and lined up his shot. Slow and deliberate he pulled the cue stick back—paused and winked at me—and made the shot.

I levelled a narrow glance at him. How long would it take for those pills to kick in? He was making some pretty impressive shots and if he won, I'd have to remove a piece of clothing.

Standing rules between Tank and I are this: in strip pool, we played best of three. When one person lost two matches, the game was called and the winner got *whatever* he, or she, wanted. I took a quick mental inventory of what I had on. Jeans, sweater, tee shirt and not much more. Maybe he'd let me take off my watch.

He dropped his seventh ball no problem and my eyes widened when he called and pocketed the eight ball, back left corner.

There were still three of my balls on the table.

I went to remove my sweater, but a tap on my arm stopped me. Tank's cue stick rested on my forearm and I followed the smooth line of the glossy stick until my gaze reached his face. Amusement shone out of his eyes as he shook his head and with the cue stick, pointed to my jeans.

"You don't get to choose. I'll take off my sweater." No way would I parade around in my underwear. Not anymore.

I slid my sweater off and draped it over the bar. So far, Plan C was not working the way I envisioned and there was no Plan D. Maintaining composure as best I could under the circumstances, I tugged my tee shirt back into place.

Because Tank won, I had to break. While I gathered the balls and arranged them in the triangle brace, Tank leaned against the bar, crossing his long muscular legs at the ankles.

Easy for him to be all relaxed, he didn't have to win two games in a row. Stifling a big yawn, I took a firm grip on the cue stick.

"I love that tee shirt," I heard him say. "We bought it in Cancun. Do you remember? That was the best two weeks ever."

Oh, I remembered all right. We went to Cancun for our honeymoon.

Gritting my teeth, I concentrated hard and hit the white cue ball dead center. When I'd finished with the follow-through, only one ball dropped. The hit had been too hard.

Tank was distracting *me*, not the other way around. Another yawn stretched through me as I chalked my cue stick and walked around, checking my options. He nursed his drink, looking like a guy who didn't have a care in the world. Looking like a guy who only had to win one more game. Those stupid pills had better start working soon since I'd just delivered a lousy break.

No matter which angle I tried, the balls were crowded too close together and there was no way to get a clean shot. As much as I hated playing 'dirty pool', I'd have to try and hook him without *looking* like I hooked him.

Tank continued reminiscing. "Yup, Cancun was a good time, but Connecticut… Now that's a holiday I'll never forget."

Whew, was it hot in here?

"I loved roughing it in Connecticut."

I gulped a big mouthful of my drink, and sucked in some ice to cool down. The heat intensified as I remembered how we 'roughed it.' After a long day hiking Tank said I'd walked through poison oak and insisted on checking me out, most thoroughly. While it turned out there had been no poison oak, not one spot on my body had been left untouched, kissed, or caressed.

"Tune him out," I muttered. "He's trying to side track you." And doing a good job.

I rolled my shoulders in a vain attempt to loosen the muscles. We both knew it was a stall tactic. Finally, I had the shot lined up, but my hand was damp and the cue stick slipped, breaking the balls wide open. Not a single ball dropped. Defeated, I stared at the brightly scattered balls like Napoleon must have done with his troops at Waterloo.

Tank pushed away from the bar and slid behind me, a solid package of heated testosterone and muscle. One large hand was placed on either side of my body, effectively boxing me in against the pool table.

"Loosen your shirt babe, I think you're time has come," he drawled against my heated cheek and dropped a kiss behind my ear.

Ripples of anticipation careened through my midsection and there wasn't much I could do except watch in dumb horror while Tank moved around the table, making impossible shots like he'd done this all his life. Complete and utter silence followed the thunk of the eight ball landing on another ball in the side pocket.

What went wrong? I have *always* played better pool than Tank and now because he won, he'd get whatever he wanted. He plucked the cue stick from my nerveless fingers and leaned it against the wall.

"Come here," he said and pulled me against his chest.

Head lowered, my forehead touching his chest, I whispered. "How did this happen? I've always won at pool."

"Yes, because I let you. It was more fun that way," he whispered against my neck as his fingers blazed a trail down my back. Warm hands pulled me close, branding me through the thin cotton. Pushing one leg between mine, there was no mistaking his intentions.

"Do you want it hard and fast, or soft and slow?" His deep voice, thick and heavy with desire, flowed over me.

"Yes," I whispered.

God help me. I wanted it all.

Chapter Six

Tank ran a hand over my rounded hip. Every inch of my skin tingled and my need for him outweighed any disappointment I'd felt at losing the game. Any hurt I'd felt when he'd left.

"Kiss me, Tank. Please." I whispered.

He lifted me onto my tiptoes and covered my mouth with his. His mouth was hungry and demanding and I kissed him back until my head swam and I was out of breath. He tore his lips from mine and lifted me onto the bar stool.

"Don't move," he warned in a low voice.

Are you kidding? I was a hot mess, quivering with need and he said don't move.

"Why?" I asked, and sucked in a breath when his fingertips feathered across my collarbone and down my arms.

"This is the soft and slow part, sweetheart."

Something akin to remorse flickered behind his eyes. I'd changed my mind. I wanted it fast and hard. And now. Did he know I wanted it now? Finally, after an eternity of waiting, he cupped my face and pressed his lips against mine and I whimpered. This unbearable need, this thirst, could only be quenched by Tank.

He drew back from the kiss and looked straight into my eyes. Hypnotized at the sight of his tongue moistening his lips, I gripped the arms of the chair and swallowed hard. He stepped back and began to unzip his jeans, then stopped.

"Is this what you were playing for?" His voice was cold, devoid of his usual humor.

A coil of unease snaked its way down my back at the question, but I was too far gone to care. I wanted him. I hopped off the bar stool and reached for his jeans.

In a blur of motion, I found myself on the pool table, large hands holding me against the rich felt cloth. With his full weight on one hand, he cradled the back of my head with the other. Raising me, he covered my mouth with his, a frantic meshing of lips, teeth and tongue, broken only when we came up for air. Then he lifted his head and looked at me. I smiled and raised my hand to caress his face, but his diamond hard eyes pierced my soul.

"Don't ever screw with me again. You want sex, just ask nice."

My hand dropped to the pool table and another part of me died, burrowing deep within my inner humiliation. He left me on the pool table and his quiet voice filtered down as he made his way to the main level. "I switched drinks with you. Sweet dreams."

Reality slammed into me as his dead tone washed me over like cold water. What had I done? Why did I think I could treat him like that? I'd take it all back if I could. Gathering my clothing, I headed upstairs. How did he know? Any dreams that he could love me again were shattered and I had no one to blame but myself.

My head felt fuzzy and I could barely put one foot in front of the other. I made it to the bedroom, dragged off my jeans and tee shirt, leaving them in a pile by the door. When I reached the bed I fell face down and was asleep before I could even crawl under the covers.

According to Plan

****

When I awoke, I found myself under the blankets; my back spooned against Tank's warm front, his arm flung over me. For a brief, quiet moment it was like the past six months never happened, and I savored the feel of his arm around me.

Thankfully, I'd drunk only a portion of the doctored rum, or I might have slept the whole day away. The room, bright with sunshine gave me sinking feeling I'd missed my alarm. Or Tank had turned it off. Either way not good, as my flight was at noon.

I eased out of Tank's grip in an attempt to see the alarm clock. If he woke before I could slip away, I'd never get out of bed. There was never a morning he hadn't awakened with an intimate agenda, which I'd happily shared. Finally, I'd inched close enough to see the time.

It was almost ten o'clock. There was no way I'd get to the airport, clear security and make my plane. Now I'd have to take a later flight or go tomorrow. First thing I had to do was call Polly, reschedule the flight— Tank's hand tightened.

Any plans to escape were doomed. He pulled me back against his solid chest, making me lose my hard-earned space. I froze in place and closed my eyes, pretending to be asleep.

"I know you're awake." He nuzzled my neck. "And I'm sorry about last night. What I did was unforgiveable. You didn't deserve my anger."

Tears pricked the back of my eyelids. Even though I was the one who tried to drug him, he was apologizing. Turning my head, ever so slightly, Tank captured my mouth with his.

"I'm sorry, too." I whispered against his mouth.

Time slowed as he gathered me close and deepened the kiss. His warm body covered mine and I smoothed my hand down his back.

"I need you, Shelby, more than you know. Will you let me show you?"

Mute, I nodded yes. I wanted this as much, if not more than him. Firm lips brushed along my collarbone and then moved lower. Much later, he covered us both with the duvet and held me tight.

Chapter Seven

I'm not sure how long I'd slept, but when I finally awakened, I stretched like a content cat in the sun, completely sated, although the killer headache lingered. I rolled out of bed and almost fell. My body wasn't used to morning calisthenics and my legs felt like rubber. Yoga, I should take yoga classes. Stay flexible and bendy. Of course, I'd have to sign Polly up with me. I wanted her tortured too.

On autopilot, I gathered my jeans and underwear draped over a chair and tossed them into the laundry basket. The black tee shirt Tank had on last night lay crumpled at the foot of my bed and I stooped to pick it up. Torn between tossing it in the room he was staying in or chucking it in the garbage, I paused. Almost against my will, I brought the shirt to my nose and inhaled his scent. I loved his cologne. In fact, I avoided the men's areas in department stores, because if I smelled this particular brand, I missed him even more.

Carefully I folded and tucked the shirt into a corner of my closet. This would be my guilty pleasure when he left.

I padded into the bathroom and had a shower, which went cold because I stood in there so long trying to shake off the effects of three sleeping pills and a couple hits of rum. When I started to brush my teeth I noticed a post-it note stuck on the mirror with Tank's distinctive handwriting scrawled across the page.

Coffee made. Omelet in microwave. T.

This show of kindness still didn't make me change my mind about letting him in on my plan. I had to find Harrison before he did. The Grants hired me to do a job and I couldn't let my personal life get in the way.

Sure enough, there was coffee in the thermos and I sat down to a well-balanced breakfast of a cheese omelet, coffee and painkillers. I took my food out to the back deck and enjoyed the fresh air. A twinge of regret flowed through me again as I remembered how cold his eyes had been. I couldn't remember a time, ever, when Tank lost his temper with me.

Not that we didn't have our differences and argue. You can't live with someone for over a year and not have some disagreements. But we'd never had a down and out fight. We didn't even raise our voices when he left me for another woman. He just walked out, leaving me stunned at the door.

The painkillers kicked in, so feeling somewhat human again, I called Polly while I grabbed a scrunchie out of my junk drawer and tied back my hair. She'd have to reschedule my flight time. The phone rang a couple of times before she answered.

"Stewart Investigations, can you hold please?"

Confused, I held the phone away from my ear and stared at it. When did we get a 'hold' button on our phone? And just how busy was Polly that she put me on hold? In less than a minute she came back on the line.

"What happened, hon? You missed your flight. Was it cancelled?"

"Long story, Polly." I continued to twist my hair into a ponytail. "Did the Grants phone back after Tank visited them?"

"No, but Regis did. You need to have a talk with him.

He's becoming a nuisance, again."

"Okay, I'll take care of it. Let me know when you've got a new flight time."

"No problem. Good luck with Regis."

Regis made my skin crawl, but out of respect for my late Aunt Tillie, who for some unknown reason liked his mother, I called. His answering machine kicked in, so I left a brief message along the lines of—I'm busy, never call back and get out of my life, just not couched in those pleasant terms.

Regis wasn't the only missing person today. Where could Tank have gone? I must have slept through him getting up and showering. I carefully opened my blinds and peeked through the front window. Tank's bike wasn't parked out front and without knowing what time he'd awakened, he could be anywhere.

In some ways I was relieved. What happened last night was downright embarrassing and I didn't want to face him yet. If he was still here when I got back from L.A., maybe we'd talk and sort a few things out. Ground rules were needed in our relationship, or whatever it was we had.

Polly called back with a re-scheduled flight time and e-mailed me my electronic boarding pass. She'd managed to book an afternoon flight and because of the time difference, it would be four o'clock local time when I arrived. Before I hung up, I gave Polly a task. I was still trying to figure out Harrison and his parent's activities prior, during and after Lulu's murder.

"I need you to check the Grant's phone records. Touch base with your contacts. See if they placed or received any calls to L.A. for the last six weeks. I also want Harrison's cell phone records for the past three months. I'll call you later tonight."

Polly's contacts throughout town were golden. She had men all over the county who loved doing favors for her. She oozed southern charm as naturally as a maple tree drips syrup. But a proverbial steel fist lay tucked inside her velvety-gloved persona. Just ask Carl Worthington, Jr. She walloped him hard when he groped her at a barn dance. I still think he swallowed the tooth that went missing.

I threw my hairbrush, moisturizer and a change of clothes into a back pack and drove to the airport, continuously looking over my shoulder for Tank. It was downright eerie how he hadn't been around. He always popped up where I least expected. A huge sigh of relief escaped me when I arrived at the terminal and boarded the plane. It was only when the doors closed and we pushed back that I realized I'd been waiting for him to come down the aisle and plunk down beside me saying something cocky, like, *'Going somewhere, darlin'?'*

I'd gotten away clean and grinned like a Cheshire cat. Finally, something had gone according to plan.

****

Tank pulled to a stop outside of Shelby's office. He'd have liked nothing better than to spend a whole day loving her. He'd lain in bed for over an hour, holding her close before she'd awakened.

I'm a fool

Last night she'd wanted him as much as he did her. There was no denying that the physical side of their marriage hadn't suffered. His only regret was that she'd started the whole strip pool game to drug him.

A small, sinking blob of undissolved powder alerted him to her plan. Switching their drinks while Shelby chose a pool cue had been simple enough. He could have easily faked drinking the rum and then pretended to sleep, but he'd been angry enough to want to teach her a lesson. He still regretted losing his temper. She didn't deserve that.

Entering the reception room of the office, the bell jangled above his head. Polly looked up and grinned. "Hi Tank. Shelby's not here."

"I know. She's back home, sleeping." He caught her quick glance at the clock and then a small frown puckered her brow. He knew Polly almost as well as he knew Shelby. Whatever plans Shelby had for today, she wasn't on time.

He'd met the two girls the same night at a local beach party. They were an unlikely pair. Polly came from old money, Shelby from need money. Polly's old man, Thaddeus B. Walker, didn't think anyone was good enough for his Southern princess. But Polly had taken to Shelby, and vice versa, their first day of school.

His difficult mission this morning was to find out what Shelby had going on. Why did she want him sound asleep? A mental kick in the pants is what he deserved, almost falling for her ruse. She'd become more devious since he'd left.

Pulling information from Polly wouldn't be easy. Although Tank kept his lines of communication open with her during the break up with Shelby, if push came to shove, Polly would side with Shelby in a heartbeat.

The phone rang and Polly looked at the call display. She answered the phone, "Stewart Investigations, can you hold please?" With a perfect smile and turning on her famed southern charm, she gushed, "Tank, would you be a doll and get me a coffee...from Hal's?"

Tank shrugged. He recognized it as a ploy to get him out of the office while she took the call. Hal's was at least four blocks away, while a perfectly good take out place was only two doors down. As the door to the office closed, he heard, "What happened, hon, you missed your flight. Was it cancelled?"

That's interesting. Shelby was flying somewhere. Now all he had to do was discover the where and when. While at Hal's, Tank bought a fresh Boston Cream donut, Polly's favorite, to go with her coffee, tossing the complimentary napkins into the garbage. The front office was empty when he got back so he placed both the donut and the coffee on her desk and snuck a glance in her tray. Seeing the top tray was empty, he rifled through papers in the second tray, yet found nothing that would tell him where Shelby was going. The only other logical place to look would have to be on the computer.

He heard Polly closing file drawers and moving around Shelby's office. Quickly he slid around and planted himself in front of her desk.

Polly, filing in her arms, came back into the reception area. "Oh, you're back. Thanks for getting me the coffee." Spotting the cream-filled treat on her desk, her eyes lit up. "Ooooh, Boston Cream." She put the files on the edge of her desk, sat down and picked the donut up.

Tank watched her take a big bite, her eyes closing as she savored the morsel.

Licking some chocolate off the corner of her mouth, she turned her keen gaze on him.

"When are you going to tell her you didn't cheat?"

Her question surprised him.

One drunken, fight-filled night he'd confessed to Polly there had been no other woman. She'd come across him picking fights in a bar and took him home to sober up.

"Funny you should ask that. The guy, who almost blew my cover, he...uh, well... Let's just say he came into his own."

"Did you kill him?" Polly's wide-eyed gaze made him laugh aloud.

"No. I didn't have to. He stepped on a few toes within his own organization and they retired him early. I have to finish the assignment I'm on right now and then there's nothing stopping me from laying it all out on the table with Shelby."

Polly gave him a thoughtful look, tapping the side of her paper cup with a perfectly manicured fingernail. "Good, because I don't like keeping secrets from her and this has been a whopper. As it is she'll probably hate me because I knew before she did."

"She'd never hate you. You're the sister she never had."

Polly finished her last bite of donut and stood. "Well, I'd give her my sister anytime. If you'll excuse me, I'll go freshen up and wash my hands. They're sticky." She proceeded down hall toward the powder room.

As soon as she was out of earshot, Tank edged around the desk, grabbed the mouse and brought up her computer desktop. Quickly scanning the screen, he noted the printer icon on the bottom right. This could only mean that Polly had recently used the printer.

Taking a chance she would be a few more minutes, he minimized the screen again and checked out the printer. A single sheet lay in the tray. A quick glance confirmed the document was a flight reservation and without looking too closely, he snapped a picture with his phone. By the time Polly returned to the reception area and her desk, he was sitting on the corner of it, finishing his coffee.

She settled back into her chair and sipped her coffee. "So, what are you really here for Tank?"

"Just wondering what Shelby's up to. Wanna fill me

in?"

Polly shook her head. "You know I can't."

"I didn't think you would, but hey, I had to try." He looked at his watch and noticed it was almost one o'clock. "Man, where has the day gone? I gotta go. See you around." He tossed his empty cup in a perfect arc, directly into the trashcan. He flashed a grin at Polly. "Two points for me."

Polly laughed and waved him out of the office. Once outside, he opened his phone and scanned the photo he'd taken. What he saw almost stopped his heart. It was now official. Shelby would send him to an early grave.

Cursing under his breath, he flipped back to his phone application and dialed his office. "Get the jet ready, I have to go to L.A." He checked his watch, "I'll be at the airport in a half-hour."

His second call was to L.A. "Dango. We have a situation. I'll be there in about three hours. Meet me at the safe house near the condo we set up as a shell for Harry, and I'll brief you."

He closed his phone and straddling his bike, throttled it to life.

You don't know what you're getting into, Shelby.

It was time to rein her in. This situation was escalating out of control. Shelby didn't know what was at stake and would get hurt if she wasn't careful. What made her think to go to L.A.? Raymond Grant must have let something slip. Tank slid on his shades and roared toward the private strip where the company plane waited.

He and Dango would stake out the condo. Knowing Shelby as well as he did, that would be one of the first places she'd go and he'd contain the situation once he got there. He hoped.

Chapter Eight

The airport in L.A. hummed with a steady cacophony of noise and people. Continually jostled from all sides, my head throbbed and I felt like a Mac truck had run over me. To top it all off, I found myself at a car rental place arguing over what my fifty dollars would get me for the day, which was almost over. This junior management executive, future pea-brain of some Fortune 500 company was adamant I pay full price.

Having no patience for this nonsense I decided it was time to bring out the big guns.

Pretending to be super-duper hot, I unzipped my hoodie and exposed the rounded tops of the 'girls'. I fanned myself with one of his pamphlets and channeled Polly. With a breathy twang, I sighed out, "Whooey! I'm not used to all this heat."

He gulped so hard I thought he'd get whiplash from his Adam's apple. I fluffed and squeezed, got great cleavage, then resumed negotiations. "So…" I looked at his nametag. "Marvin. Where were we?"

He never knew what hit him. Twenty minutes later I wheeled out of the airport parking lot driving a sporty Jeep truck with two days of unlimited mileage for thirty-five dollars. I had no qualms using my 'assets' to get what I needed.

Within reason.

Before checking into the hotel I cruised around looking for a good costume store. I didn't know who else may be looking for Harrison so I wanted to be almost invisible to anyone staking the place out. I figured I'd go with a hooker ensemble. No one noticed streetwalkers. They became part of the scenery and you only saw them when they let you. Also, Harry was known to have liked cheap tarts and I would just be another girl from the street.

I almost missed the costume place. A tacky little shop, it lay tucked between two taller buildings that leaned toward each other like a couple of drunken sailors. Next earthquake, even a 2.0, would make them topple. How they passed safety inspections baffled me. With that thought in mind, I rushed in, bought what I needed and got out of there.

In case the front desk clerk of my hotel spotted me, I changed in the main floor bathroom and then slipped out one of the back exits. A big wig, passion-pit red lipstick, tight dress, and three-inch stilettos completed my disguise. The nightlife of downtown Hollywood was vibrant and I blended in beautifully.

****

Driving slowly down the street, I kept a sharp eye out for Harrison's address. Big palm trees, flashy cars and the brilliance of neon lights distracted me. Getting lost would have been easy. The streets became narrower and more dingy the closer I got to his address.

Most hookers didn't own sport utility vehicles, so I parked a few blocks from Harrison's apartment building, down a narrow back alley. Before getting out of my vehicle I made sure I had the key to Harrison's apartment and a can of pepper spray in my purse. Not wanting to lose my hotel swipe card and driver's license, in case someone mugged me, I locked them into the glove box.

Feigning nonchalance, I casually strolled to Harrison's apartment building, unlocked the front door and entered. No one noticed me and I let go of the breath I didn't realize I'd been holding and moved to the elevator. I pressed the up key a few times before noticing a sign with sloppy letters advising the elevator was broken and a hand drawn arrow pointed to a door at the end of the hall and fire escape.

Fortunately for me, Harrison lived on the second floor. There was no way I could have walked six or seven stories in these shoes and I wasn't taking them off for anyone. I had no idea who or what had been on these stairs, or who had done what in this stairwell.

I reached his apartment and after struggling with the lock, pushed open the door. Surprisingly, Harrison's condo was spacious and bright. And I mean *very* spacious, as in empty. Not a dish, curtain, or stick of furniture.

Clacking my way into the kitchen in my stilettos—*who makes these shoes anyway?*—I grabbed the first drawer and pulled it open. Peering into it didn't reveal anything taped against the counter top so I gingerly felt under each and every drawer (all four of them). *Please don't let there be a spider.* And I cringed a lot, not wanting to touch anything I might regret.

Maybe there was something in the bathroom. In the movies, there were always packages of important papers wrapped in protective plastic. But no hidden surprises there either and his bedroom contained no clues. I made my way back to the living room and stood, hands on hips, surveying the apartment as a whole. It looked like no one had lived here in a long time.

Harrison's mysterious disappearance had taken an

interesting turn. When you eliminated everything probable all that's left was the improbable. It was beginning to look like Harrison had been moved...by experts. The question remained—willing or unwilling?

The second probability, and the one I suspected as bang on, was that Harrison had never lived here. This place was cleaner than a brand new whistle. A complete dead-end and I had no idea what to tell the Grants. I decided to go back to the hotel. Tomorrow I'd try to find some hookers who knew Lulu and with any luck, Harrison.

I re-locked the apartment and exited the building and had gone only a few steps when a familiar flashing red light bounced off the grimy walls of the adjoining building. Sure enough, I turned around and an unmarked squad car glided to a stop, the little flashing light perched precariously on the dash. Must be a quiet night if I'm the one they're stopping and not the actively working ladies of the night. But then again, I was a new girl on this street and they could just be checking me out. I waited for the cop to get out of his car.

A rugged plain-clothes cop unfolded himself from the driver's seat, a badge clipped to his belt. The subdued lighting in the alley made it difficult to see if anyone else was with him. The cop approached with a polite smile on his face.

"Do you have identification, ma'am?" he said with a pleasant Australian accent.

"No, I don't have any on me, officer, it's in my vehicle." I tried my best to be demure. Hard to do when the dress left nothing to the imagination, but the last thing I needed was to cause trouble and bring attention to myself.

"Would you please face the wall and keep your hands where I can see them." I shrugged, turned around and waited... and waited. I looked from side to side. *Jose loves*

Maria was scrawled on the side of a building in broad loopy letters. Some kind of green goo slid down the wall from a second story window. I did *not* want to know what it could be.

As I shifted from one foot to the other, the balls of my feet aching in these stupid shoes, I head a car door open and a heated, whispered conversation. I strained everything I had to hear what they were saying. The car door opened and closed again.

The cop cleared his throat. "Ma'am, I'm going to have to take you downtown."

Why would Crocodile Dundee take me downtown?

I turned and faced him. "For what cause? Wearing uncomfortable shoes?"

He took my arm at the wrist and elbow and led me to the back of the cruiser.

"Wait, what about my rights?" A bubble of panic rose in my throat and I tugged against his grip. What if he wasn't a cop and this was an elaborate ruse to kidnap me into a sex trade ring? The unmarked car looked legit, but anybody could buy a flashing red light and slap a fake badge onto their belt.

"We'll discuss that at the station." He took a firmer hold on my arm.

Tugging again I said, "This is wrong. You have no grounds."

I tried to twist and grab my purse which kept swinging out of reach. My intention was to pull out the pepper spray, as I'd lost the element of surprise and couldn't flip him. Plus, there was a second person waiting in the car. My stomach went into free fall.

"I could say you're resisting arrest and causing a disturbance. Now be quiet and get in the car." With his hand covering the back of my head so it wouldn't bang the doorframe, he pushed me into the rear seat. Panicked, I could only watch as he climbed into the front of the car.

What just happened? My heart hammered in my chest a million miles per minute. Why hadn't I screamed? Why hadn't I done a more defensive move and disabled him? Although frantic, I pulled the purse onto my lap and slowly tugged at the zipper, hoping they wouldn't hear me. It was then I smelled peppermint.

"Get me out of this car, now!" I pulled on the door handle, as well as kicked the back of the seat where Tank sat. I felt immense satisfaction when my heel pierced the leather. "What gives you the right?"

We drove three or four blocks before backtracking to the alley where my rental was parked. Furious over this new turn of events, I think I had a mental breakdown. Tank exited the car and came around to open my door. A red haze misted over my eyes and in slow motion I reached into the purse, closed my hand around the little silver canister of pepper spray, and waited, my index finger twitching on the nozzle.

He leaned down and held out his hand to help me out of the back of the car. Whipping out the can of pepper spray, I hit the button. Instead of a broad mist, a thin stream squirted out and hit him beside the eye. Tank instinctively stumbled back, which gave me a chance to push by him and make a run for my car. As I fumbled with the purse to find my keys, I realized— too late—I was running in three-inch stilettos.

The sound of pounding feet echoed behind me. Air whooshed out of my lungs when he tackled and twisted in mid-air so I wouldn't get crushed when we landed. My legs swung in an arc, like a pendulum. One shoe sailed through the air, landing somewhere past the back of my vehicle. We hit the ground with a thud and he flipped again, pinning me under his body. I pushed the wig out of my eyes and wriggled around until I lay on my back.

His red-rimmed green eye watered where the spray had caught, and a muscle clenched along his jaw line. The only tell-tale sign he was angry. Maybe beyond angry. Any sane person would be. I'd doctored his drink not more than twenty-four hours ago, pepper sprayed him, and tried to run away.

When he released his hold and stood, I fully expected him to berate me like a child. I almost didn't accept the hand he held out.

"You all right, mate?" His buddy called out from the cruiser as I rose to a standing position.

Without turning, Tank nodded. "Yup. Thanks, Dango."

I pulled my hand from Tank's grip. "What is this all about?"

I heard the Dundee's car reverse and he left us there to scrap it out. Smart cop.

"I figured you were up to something, so I talked to Polly." He crossed his arms across his chest and continued to glare down at me. "I flew here and waited. We thought we'd give you a scare, teach you a lesson."

"I didn't need to be taught a lesson. You don't have to babysit me." A slow boil of anger started in my belly. I stepped back, continuing to brush and pick garbage off my clothes.

"Are you sure? Dango's eyes almost popped out of their socket when he saw you. What *are* you doing in this outfit anyway?"

"Harrison likes call girls. I figured neighbors wouldn't notice a new hooker going to his place." I shrugged my shoulders. "You know, hide in plain sight."

Realizing I had only one shoe on, I removed the

strappy, torture device and looked around for the other one. It probably was in the pile of garbage behind my car. No way would I go back there to find it. There could be rats, or worse – spiders. The shoe could rot there.

Tank uncrossed his arms and took a step in my direction. "You could have gotten hurt. What if it hadn't been *me* in that car? What if it had been some psycho jerk wad with his paws all over you? Did you even think about that?" His voice grew louder. "You need a handler."

The anger within bubbled up a bit more. There was no way I'd tell Tank those very same thoughts crossed my mind.

"I don't need anybody," I yelled back, jutting my chin forward. The wig fell into my eyes again, which proved to be the last straw. Mount Shelby erupted. Every frustration, every hurt I'd suffered because of him coursed through my voice. I pushed the wig out of my eyes and we stood toe to toe, nose to… sternum.

"I can take care of myself! I've been doing great since you left." We both knew I meant more than my job and this recent escapade.

"You still need a handler!" Tank bit out.

I shook my head and turned toward my vehicle. Truth be told, what happened in the alley had scared me right down to the bottom of my sore feet.

I'd go back to the hotel, call Polly and check in. Tomorrow I'd locate some hookers who may have known Lulu and Harry. And then—I paused in my thoughts—then I was having my head examined.

"I'm outta here." I called over my shoulder to Tank. He could find his own way back to wherever it was he was staying.

He muttered behind me, "Well, if that's the way it's got

to be, then okay."

I didn't even have a chance to squeak before I was tossed over his shoulder like a sack of flour, one large hand spread across my derriere. He rifled through my purse, which swung with each angry stride and pulled out the car keys. Before cramming his big frame into the driver's side, he unceremoniously dumped me into the passenger seat. He stopped only long enough to ask me where I was staying and then revving the motor, tore up the alley and raced toward my hotel.

****

The desk clerk's jaw dropped and his eyes opened wide when we barreled through the lobby. Tank, grim-faced, carried the back pack and I stomped alongside barefoot. One shoe dangled from my fingers, the other lay forgotten in the alley. Hotel guests stared openly and gave us a wide berth. Probably because we looked like a hillbilly wedding gone bad.

The ride in the elevator was strained, to say the least and after I unlocked the door I stormed into the room, not caring if Tank followed. He threw my bag on the bed and I made a beeline for the bathroom, slammed the door and locked it.

Standing in front of the mirror I stared at my reflection. The wig lay twisted to one side, looking like a bird's nest with twigs and bits of paper sticking out and the garish makeup had rubbed off in patches. I stripped, throwing the clothes in the garbage while waiting for the tub to fill. Once it was ready I slid into the hot water and lay there, staring at the ceiling.

I scrubbed the makeup off my face, turning the white cloth into a rainbow of colors and thought about Tank. He'd been sending off so many mixed signals, I had no idea what he was doing or where I stood with him. It was frustrating how he magically turned up wherever I went.

I sat up, water splashing over the side of the tub. How *did* he get to Harrison's place before me? Closing my eyes, I recalled what he said in the alley. He said he'd been waiting and watched me go into Harrison's building. He also said he was at my office when Polly booked my flight and I knew he hadn't been on the same flight, because I'd looked. How did he know where I'd go, and more importantly, how did he get to LA so fast? The only plausible answer was private transportation.

Fast, expensive transportation.

Now I itched in *my* don't-wanna-itch-place.

Chapter Nine

Lying in the tub, I wished I had my iPod. Then it would drown any and all sounds of Tank in the other room. I didn't want any reminders that he had once again ended up in the same place as me.

How did he know exactly where I'd be? Was he following me to find Harrison? I quickly discarded that thought as it didn't make sense and he'd said 'they waited for me'. Although I was angry at Tank, I knew he was good at his job and had no reason to trail me. What should have been a simple missing person's case was turning out to be not so simple.

I felt like a chubby rodent on a stationary wheel.

First order of business was to call Polly and find out how Tank knew I was in L.A. So, after drying off I wrapped a hotel robe around me and head held high, walked into the other room where Tank reclined on one of the double beds. I'd pretend he wasn't there, the big interloper.

Curled in the wingback chair, my legs tucked beneath me, I called Polly's home phone. There was no answer so I had to leave a message.

"Hi Polly, it's me. Guess who's in L.A.? Give you three guesses and if one of them's Tank, you win the prize. Okay, gotta go now. Oh, and Polly? If I find out you told him what I was doing, you are *so* fired." I replaced the phone receiver with a decisive click. Let her stew on that for a while. I glared at Tank when I thought I heard a choked chuckle, but his face remained stoic and he seemed mesmerized by the football game on TV.

I sniffed in disdain and went back into the bathroom to blow-dry my hair and moisturize.

About an hour later, I phoned a second time. Still no answer. I tapped the receiver against my chin. This was Thursday night and Polly never missed her TV shows. She'd better not be screening her calls. Tank, by this time had fallen asleep and was snoring lightly.

Time to get down and dirty. The next attempt went straight through to her answering machine. In case she *was* monitoring calls I said, with saccharine sweetness, "Hi. It's me, again. You're still fired. And since you won't talk to me now, I have lots and lots of time to call Regis. I think I'll start by telling him you've had a secret crush on him for years and—"

Polly picked up. "Now that's just mean. I'd never do that to you. You're like a sister to me."

"Stuff it. You hate your sister."

"Well, if I had a sister I liked, it would be you."

I snorted. "How did Tank know I was here?"

"I don't know. I didn't tell him anything. In fact, when you called, I sent him to Hal's for coffee." That explained why she put me on hold. "So how could he...? Oh, dang! He was alone in the office when I went to the powder room."

"Well, he must have found something because he was outside Harry's apartment waiting, and now he's here in the hotel with me." I turned away from the bed and lowered my voice. "Did you get the other thing we talked about?" Even though it looked like Tank was asleep, I couldn't take the chance he wasn't. I didn't want him to know I'd asked Polly to dig up phone records for me.

"My boy at the phone company says he should have them tomorrow. Is Tank coming back with you?" She sounded hopeful.

I looked over at Tank. His eyes were closed.

"Nope, he's on his own."

"Oh." Polly sounded disappointed. "Do you want me to change your flight to tomorrow morning then?"

I picked up my airline ticket and checked the flight time.

"No, leave it for the afternoon. Tomorrow after breakfast I'm going to the area where Lulu may have worked. With luck, I'll find some working girls that knew her and get some answers. I should be home around eight o'clock. Why don't you come by the house then?" I said good-bye, and hung up.

My stomach growled. Realizing I hadn't eaten in almost ten hours, I decided to grab a bite from the little deli I'd noticed beside the hotel. I glanced over to the bed, and Tank.

"Tank?"

No response. Still peeved at what happened earlier I didn't even try to wake him. Back pack in hand, I went into the bathroom and changed. In less than five minutes, I quietly closed the bathroom door, grabbed my hotel swipe card and headed for the elevators.

When I returned about a half an hour later, there was no sign of Tank but a note lay on the pillow. *We'll talk later. Love you. T.* I read the note, then crumpled the scrap of paper and tossed it in the garbage can. He wasn't back in my good books with one lousy note.

I sat on the bed for about five minutes before reaching back into the trash can. Pulling out the note, I smoothed it out and traced the words *Love you* with my fingertip. I then carefully folded the paper and tucked it into my back pocket. I didn't even try to reason why I wanted to keep it safe. That was just one more thing to keep me from sleeping.

****

Next morning I woke up stiffer than a starched shirt. Playing tackle football in the back alley had me walking around almost bent at the waist. Polly and I would absolutely take yoga classes. My few toiletries were thrown back into my bag and then I checked out. I had less than four hours to find some of the working girls Harrison liked.

Mid-afternoon in Hollywood was hot and sticky. There was no hope for me as my hair curled out of control in the humidity and any deodorant I might have put on that morning had long evaporated. I slid off my hoodie and tied it around my waist. That was better, although my tee shirt clung like a second skin.

Two women approached. The taller one, a statuesque black woman, looked me over from head to toe. She balanced a cheroot in one of those long, slender cigarette holders at the end of her fingers. She could have been a black Joan Crawford with her pencil-thin eyebrows and ruby red lipstick. The only difference being, Miss Crawford would never have gone out in public wearing a figure-hugging tube dress completed by faux leather boots zipped over her knees. She blew concentric circles of smoke into the air before asking, "You new here?"

"This is our corner." The second hooker piped up. The inflection in her voice told me she was a girl from North Dakota, doncha know. Petite and curvaceous, she had massive auburn ringlets and big, wide-spaced hazel eyes.

"No, I'm not from here. I'm looking for anyone who knew a girl who worked around here. You may have known her... Lulu?"

I thought I saw a slight hesitation from the black woman, but she quickly replied, "Honey, all the girls here are Lulu, or Fiona, or Pussy Galore. Who do you want us to be?"

"No, *I'm* not looking for a girl, I mean, I am... Wait, let's start over. I'm looking for anyone who knew Lulu. She was murdered and the cops think it was a john called Harry. Ring any bells?"

The black woman stiffened noticeably. "You a cop?"

"No. I'm a private investigator." I pulled out my business cards and handed one to her. "I've been hired by Harry's family to find him. Did you know Lulu or Harry?"

They both looked at the card, caution evident on their faces. It became pretty obvious I needed to gain a bit of their trust. "Look, I'm not here to cause trouble. I'm just trying to figure out why the cops think Harry killed Lulu and where he could have gone."

The black woman handed back the card. "Sorry honey, we cain't help you."

They started to walk away. They couldn't leave, they knew something. I could feel it in my bones. In desperation, I called out. "How much?"

Grabbing my wallet out of my back pack I pulled out some bills and waved them. North Dakota girl grabbed my still-waving hand and hissed, "Put it away. You get seen passing money on the street and you'll get arrested faster than you can spit."

"I can get arrested for a lot less and faster than that." I said drily and tucked my wallet into my bag. "All I want is information. What are your names anyway? I hate talking to people when I don't know their name.

"I'm... Carla," The black woman responded. "And this

is Desiree."

Desiree waved.

"Thanks. So did you know Lulu?"

"Yeah, we knew her," Carla said.

Desiree, seemingly bored with the conversation, drifted to the edge of the sidewalk and smiled at slow-cruising cars. One vehicle, with dark tinted windows, stopped and she leaned toward the window. I heard her ask if they were looking for a date.

I directed my questions to Carla. "Was Harry good to Lulu?"

"Oh yeah. He sure was sweet on her." Carla chewed her gum and nodded at another dark, low-slung sedan. Once the car slid by, she turned her attention back to me. "He always bought stuff, treated her real good."

"Yah," Desiree, back with us for the moment, interrupted. "He was always buying her stuff. She showed me some of the clothes and jewelry. I told her she should hock some. He gave her really good stuff. Poor Lulu. Wouldn't sell none of it. Said she loved him."

"Oh man, remember that bracelet." Carla rolled her eyes and lit another cheroot. She blew a perfect 'o' ring over my head. "It had to put him back at least five G's. I wonder what happened to all that stuff." She looked over at Desiree, "Do you think Chester got it?"

"Who's Chester?" I blurted out.

"Her pimp." Desiree replied.

Carla took another drag off her cheroot. "Yeah, good 'ole Chester would've cleaned out her whole place. There be none of her stuff around no more."

"Would Harry have killed Lulu?"

"No way he sliced and diced her." Carla's voice was firm. "He was going to get her out of this place. It was one sick dude who offed Lulu."

This didn't make any sense. Why would the cops think Harrison had done the dirty deed? The hamster-on-the-wheel feeling intensified. "Do you have any idea where Harry could have gone?"

Carla arched an eyebrow and sneered. "What do I look like, his mother?"

Desiree snickered and they high-fived each other. Then, bored expressions on their faces, they turned in silent unison and strolled down the sidewalk away from me. It was as if they had never stopped and talked.

Dejected, I took the rental back to the airport and caught my flight home. The trip to L.A. had been a waste of time.

****

Five long hours later I slouched up the front steps of my house and inserted the key into the door. I heard someone on the steps behind me. No hesitation this time, I slid my hand into my purse in the back pack. Armed with pepper spray, I turned. Not an intruder, but the temptation to spray the weasel at the foot of my steps was overwhelming.

"Regis, you almost gave me a heart attack! What are you doing here anyway?"

Regis lived three doors down. He either sprinted here or had been hiding in the rhododendrons. I went with the flowers. He couldn't run that fast. I dropped the canister back into my bag although I wanted to still spray him. That might stop him from bothering me.

"Good evening, Shelby." He adjusted his glasses. "Mother is most anxious that I return some items which belonged to your late Aunt Matilda."

"Does it have to be now? I just got back and I'm bagged."

"This will not take much of your time. Mother wanted me to bring you these recipes your Aunt Matilda lent her. She forgot about them when she moved to Shady Pines." He stood on the first step and handed me an envelope with Aunt Tillie's spidery handwriting on the outside.

This was what he'd been pestering me for? Here I thought he was going to ask me out again.

"Uh...thanks. This means a lot to me." I edged closer to my door. He took another step, cleared his throat and slicked back his hair with the palm of his hand. Inwardly, I cringed, knowing what could be coming next.

"I am taking Mother to the Museum of Natural History this weekend and wondered if you might care to join us?" Perspiration dotted his upper lip and he cleared his throat again.

"I... Ahhh..."

"She's already got a date, sonny boy." I pivoted to my left and watched Tank's long stride eat up the sidewalk.

"I thought you were in L.A.," Regis sputtered, shrinking away.

"Just got back and couldn't wait to get home to the little woman." Tank gave me an intimate, dangerous smile.

If I hadn't been so creeped out by the fact Regis was here, I'd have told him exactly what he could do with his sexy smile, long legs and muscular arms.

Regis further stepped back when Tank came up on the porch and wrapping those muscular arms around my waist, twirled me around. Mid twirl, he claimed my mouth and set me down. Strong teeth nipped my lower lip and he gave it a gentle tug. All I could do was hold onto his biceps as I swayed into his body and returned the kiss.

When he stepped back, I caught a dangerous glint in his eye when his gaze fixed heatedly on my now swollen lower lip. I got his message loud and clear. *Mine*. He left his armed draped across my shoulders and turned and faced Regis.

"Thanks for dropping by." Tank reached out and gave him a handshake and I'm sure I heard bones crack. "Nice that you're all neighborly, but I gotta get Shelby in the house before she faints from hunger, right sweetheart?"

Still a bit bemused by the kiss, I could only nod yes.

Regis mumbled his goodbye and retreated toward his house. I looked at Tank and ducked under his arm through my open door, intending to lock him out. His big boot on the threshold prevented it, so I flounced, yes, I flounced into the kitchen. My equilibrium was returning.

I'll sweetheart him in a minute.

Mentally I prepared myself for a full frontal attack from Tank. I waited...and waited. No Tank. Where was he now? For all I knew he could be peeing in corners, further staking out his territory.

I walked back to the entrance of the kitchen. Down the hall near the front door Tank stood staring at a framed photo on the wall. The picture was of him, Aunt Tillie, my mom and I, taken on a family vacation. We stood smiling, arms around each other with the beautiful mountains of Virginia as our backdrop.

Tank had an old army buddy there he wanted to see, so we three girls opted to stay in the small city about an hour from his friend's ranch. We'd had manicures, pedicures and shopped until we dropped. It had been our last vacation together and this photo was the only one with my mom and Aunt Tillie together with me, so I never removed it from the wall.

"I always liked your mom and aunt. They were like family to me."

I knew that. Aunt Tillie had been almost as devastated

as me when Tank left. The kicker was she hadn't stayed mad, like me. Both she and Polly had a soft spot for him and wouldn't let me out-and-out hate him. I grabbed my bag and headed upstairs with Tank following. Halfway up I stopped and turned. Although two steps behind, he remained eye level with me.

"Oh no, cowboy." I jabbed a finger in his shoulder. "You lost your chance to stay here. Get out and find some other woman to haunt. We're through."

"Darlin', it's my house too. But if it makes you feel any better, I promise on my mother's grave I will not lay a hand on you until you ask." He placed his right hand over his heart. "I'll stay in our guest room, cross my heart, hope to die, stick a—"

"Shame on you," I interrupted. "You told me your mother was alive and well, counting cards in Vegas."

He sidestepped me and bounded up the stairs, throwing an unrepentant grin over his shoulder. "I know, but it worked."

The guest bedroom door slammed shut.

Chapter Ten

My first instinct when I got to my bedroom was to crawl into bed, pull the covers over my head and hide from the world for a day or two. But Aunt Tillie always said, *Child, it's better to meet life head on than waitin' for it to sneak up from behind. That way it can't bite you in the 'you know where.'*

Then she'd laugh and threaten to show me all the bite marks she'd received from life. Aunt Tillie was my mother's aunt. She'd come to live with me when mom became sick and stayed until she passed. Tragically, a short time later, Aunt Tille was struck by a car on her way home from shopping. I lost both my mom and Great Aunt within months of each other.

Sometimes I missed them both so much it felt like a canyon stretched where my heart used to be. At one time Tank filled that huge void. Then he took off and the ditch widened even more.

The doorbell chimed and I hastily wiped the tears off my cheeks. Taking deep breaths, I willed myself to get a grip before going downstairs. I opened the door to Polly, who held a bag of nacho chips in one hand and a bottle of wine in the other. The cloying scent of *Poison*, by Dior, wafted on the air as she breezed by.

"Do you put that stuff on by the gallon or what?" I

waved a hand in front of my face to disperse the air a bit.

"Put what on?" She blithely continued down the hall to my kitchen.

"Your perfume. Geez, Polly. There's a red haze following you and dogs are crying next door because they can't breathe." I followed and watched her pull out a big bowl for chips, then glasses for the wine. I noticed she brought down three glasses.

"Polly, you didn't come by here to see Tank, did you?"

"Who me?" She batted innocent eyes. "Now why would I do that?'

I snorted in disbelief.

"I stopped to find out how your little trip went and to give you these." She pulled a sheaf of papers from her Fendi bag with phone numbers, times and dates on it. "Gorgeous, hunky man staying at your house had no bearing what-so-ever that I wore my new sweater. You like?"

Polly had on a soft pink sweater, which showed off her Mae West figure to perfection as she swayed into the living room with the wine. Sway was the only way to describe Polly's walk. She just kind of 'sashayed.' You almost expected her to put a hand on her hip and ask you to come over sometime. She made me smile, as always.

Papers in hand, I grabbed the bowl of nachos and headed into the living room. Focused on the pages I didn't watch where I was going and tripped over Tank's long legs, stretched out from the couch. He shot out an arm and caught me. Stiffening, I placed the nachos on the coffee table, moved away from him and sat in my easy chair.

Polly settled in next to Tank and offered him a glass. They immediately started laughing and joking. I was so jealous of their camaraderie I could have spit nails, so I pretended to study the phone list.

Tank kept looking over to me and I knew he wondered what Polly had given me, so I lifted the sheet higher to hide my smug smile. The first page had lots of phone calls to local numbers and I could see the L.A. prefix interspersed among them. I was about to check out the next page when Polly piped up.

"So, what did the hookers have to say?"

I lowered the sheets of paper and glared, willing her to realize I hadn't said anything to Tank about talking to hookers.

She caught my glare. "What?"

Tank looked from me to Polly and back at me again. "What hookers?"

He sat up straight on the couch and leaned toward me. "Did you do anything that could have gotten you hurt, or in trouble?"

"More trouble than getting arrested outside an apartment?" I quipped.

Polly choked on her sip of wine. "You were arrested?"

"No. Tank and Crocodile Dundee bulldozed me into a police cruiser and then we went for a ride."

"I was just looking out for your best interests. And I forgive you for pepper spraying me."

I felt heat steal across my cheeks.

"You pepper sprayed Tank?" Polly's eyes widened and she put her wine on the coffee table. She twisted to face him and touched his arm. "Tank, you poor thing, are you okay?"

My eyes narrowed as I watched her console poor, poor Tank. What was she up to?

He nodded, but kept his gaze on me. "So fill me in. What did you find out in L.A.?" Leaning back once more, he put both arms on the back of the couch and kicked his feet out onto the coffee table. "Maybe we can bounce ideas off each other and figure out where he's gone."

Polly picked up her wine glass and settled into the corner of the couch, tucking her feet under her bottom. It was then I noticed her wink at me as she took a sip of wine and watched the two of us. Oh no. She was playing matchmaker. Give me a gun and let me shoot myself.

"Shelby, what did you find out?" Tank's question stopped me from throttling Polly.

I paused and went back over my day. "This morning I talked to a couple of hookers who might have known Lulu. They don't believe Harrison is the murderer. They're street savvy and if they don't think he did the deed, then, my gut says they're bang on. So... I have to ask myself, why has Harrison disappeared? Does he think he's being framed? Is he a target as well?"

Visualizing Harrison's apartment I stood, tucked the folded papers into my back pocket, and began to pace. I did my best thinking when I wasn't sitting still.

"His place was too sterile. Made me think he hadn't lived there. Or, almost like it had been professionally cleaned. Most people forget something, like a bar of soap, razor blade. Little things that we just think, *'Let the other guy have it, I'm outta here.'* Nope, Harrison is a real mystery."

Tank stroked his strong jaw, nodding. "You may be right. Dango didn't say Harry was the killer, only that he was a person of interest. He disappeared right after the murder."

I kept musing out loud. "I wonder why he thought he had to go into hiding. And who's bankrolling it? Harrison didn't pay his own bills, there's no way he could keep afloat and try to stay out of sight." A huge yawn escaped me and my eyelids felt like sandpaper. "I'll look closer at his parents. They might have hired me to create the illusion of

Harry taking a walk."

Tank's hand paused as he reached for a chip and he shot a hard look at me. A little puzzled by it, but too exhausted to figure out why, I yawned again and stretched. After running on about six hours of sleep over the past two days, my personal gas tank hit empty. I had to get some sleep.

With another big stretch I looked over at Polly and Tank talking. They'd always had an easy friendship. Disgusted with my envy of Polly I decided to get out of there before I said something I'd regret, again.

"Good night."

Did they even notice me leave? I headed down the hall and heard Tank's deep voice ask Polly if she'd like more wine. Trudging up the stairs I wanted that to be me on the couch, laughing and teasing with him. The one thing Tank and I lost, along with trust, was having fun.

Nightly rituals completed, I finally crawled into bed. For at least an hour I tossed and turned, frustrated that I couldn't fall asleep no matter how tired I was. Through the vents I heard talking and the tinkle of Polly's laughter. Bitter jealousy tightened around my heart, squeezing until I felt physical pain. If I had a heart attack and died, would they miss me?

Probably not.

Hands grab at me, pulling me toward a big crate. I hear the cries of women from within, calling out to be released. I try to stop them. I don't want to be sold into slavery.

I awoke with a start, my heart racing. Even though I was a little disoriented, the dream remained vivid in my mind. I glanced at the alarm clock which dimly glowed a few minutes after two o'clock a.m. A bit shaken, I stared at my bedroom door, and willed Tank to come through it.

I'd never admit that his scare tactic in L.A. had worked

but it would be nice if he'd wrap his arms around me and keep me safe.

The door remained closed and a tiny ache settled around my heart. Why did I think he'd come to my room after promising to leave me alone? I guess I never expected him to keep his word, at least not when it came to sleeping with me.

Slipping out of bed, I tiptoed across the room, opened the door slowly, crept across the hall and pressed my ear to the guest bedroom door. What did I think I was going to hear? Polly and Tank getting it on. I froze at the thought. They wouldn't. Would they?

I opened the door a crack and listened again. Tank's gentle snoring was all I heard. I eased the door open further, poked my head in and looked around toward his bed.

From the light of a street lamp, filtered through gauzy curtains, I saw him spread out, blankets all tangled, his arm flung over the edge of the bed. I edged in a little further. As I got closer I confirmed he was alone and a deep sigh breathed out of me from relief. I turned to sneak back out and stumbled against the bed. I ducked low, hoping he wouldn't see me.

"Trouble sleeping?"

I knew by the inflection in his voice, he was trying not to laugh. Embarrassed at getting caught, I stood, prepared to brazen it out.

"Thought I heard a noise and came in to make sure you were okay," I lied and turned to leave.

"Wait," he called out, his voice deep and husky from sleep. "Stay with me."

"I don't think that's a good idea."

"To sleep only, darlin'. I miss having you next to me. And besides, I promised I wouldn't lay a hand on you unless you asked."

I looked over my shoulder and felt so torn. The logical side of my brain said, 'get out, don't make a bigger fool of yourself'. But the mushy heart side, the one that needed him, shouted, 'stay, stay, stay'.

My heart was a traitor to my mind.

"Okay, if you insist." I crawled over him, into the bed. "Don't think this makes up for arresting me in L.A."

"Didn't think it would" He wrapped his arms around me and I curled against his chest, twining my legs with his. "Go to sleep, you'll feel better in the morning."

The steady rhythm of his breathing and heart soothed me. Through my hair I felt a feather light kiss and he pulled me in a little closer. God, I loved this man.

Within minutes, I was sound asleep.

Sue Barr

Chapter Eleven

...his mouth follows the curve of my collarbone before sliding up to capture my lips. Instinctively I arch, and push up against his hard body. One hand caresses my thigh while the alarm clock rings, and rings, and rings....

My hand groped around the nightstand, searching for the alarm clock. It took a few more rings before I realized the 'alarm' was actually a cell phone. Who would call this early in the morning? I found the offending phone and glared at it. All the call display showed was unknown number, so I hit talk and held it to my ear.

A disembodied voice droned, "Enter the four digit code from your computer."

What the...? I held the phone out and studied the unfamiliar icons. Rubbing sleep out of my eyes, I looked again. Uh oh, not my phone, it was Tank's. I punched end and dropped his phone back onto the nightstand. Simultaneously, I remembered I was in the guest bedroom. The same guest bedroom and bed where Tank slept and where coincidentally I happened to be all cozy beneath the duvet.

Groaning softly, I flopped back onto the pillow and I covered my eyes with the back of my hand, flushing at the memory of using Tank as my personal body pillow. I pushed the duvet off and sat. Where was Tank anyway? The deep baritone of Tank singing, *I Love This Bar*, filtered down the hall. A giggle slipped past me.

He only sang Toby Keith in the shower when he was in a good mood. This was almost always followed by a gourmet spread of French toast, crisp bacon and the best coffee in the state.

I wasn't ready to face him yet. Not after practically begging to let me sleep with him. So much for the hands-off message I'd instigated. I skidded into my bedroom and fell back against the closed door. I pushed away from the door and had my own solitary shower. Heat unfurled within me at the thought of Tank naked in the other shower. I dropped my head against the cool tile. Oh, how I wanted to skip my dripping body down the hall and surprise him like the good old days. The pull to join him was so strong my stomach churned. I had to get my thoughts and hormones under control. A friggin' yo-yo bounced around less than I did.

Although I wanted to, in a bad, bad way, I didn't jump Tank. I finished my shower and proceeded to pull on clean jeans and a tee shirt that said, '*If you don't like my attitude now, you won't like it later*'. The scent of fresh coffee and the mouth-watering bacon floated into the bedroom while I dressed for work. I'd never admit it to him, but I missed his cooking.

What would I say to him over breakfast? He didn't know I'd had this great epiphany before I fell asleep. And I wasn't ready to be the first one to say 'I love you.' Not after what he had done. He left me, not the other way around. I expected some major groveling from the boy.

Once dressed, I walked over to my dresser and put on my watch. As I hooked the clasp I glanced over the phone bills I'd left lying there. The ones Polly brought over last night. Smoothing out the paper, I examined the long list, turning to the second page. A series of phone calls made to a familiar number practically jumped off the page and alarm bells rang.

Why were the Grants calling Tank?

This tidbit of information was something I hadn't expected. Harrison's disappearance took another fascinating turn. In fact, going by this print out, they had been calling Tank for several months. My previous suspicions that this whole business had been too coincidental were confirmed by this list. I ticked off on my fingers all Tank 'coincidences.'

1. He'd shown up right after I was hired by Raymond Grant.

2. He'd been waiting for me at the end of their drive.

3. He'd been camped outside Harrison's apartment.

I looked again at the list and a harsh realization floored me. They must have told him I was going to LA. Why would they hire me when they could have hired Tank? And why would Tank be talking to them if he suspected Harrison murdered a girl in LA?

I needed some uninterrupted time to figure this out and the best place would be my office, alone. I grabbed the list, ran down the stairs and yelled out, "See you later." I thought I heard Tank call out, "Wait!" but ignored him and couldn't help but feel like a guilty husband ducking out on the loving wife, slaving over breakfast.

My drive to work would normally take anywhere from ten to fifteen minutes. This morning however, there was a detour on the main road. I followed the temporary road signs while listening to my favorite country music station. Consumed with thoughts of the phone records, the Grants and what possible link they could have to Tank, I didn't notice that over time and a few right turns, the only car traveling down this narrow side road was mine.

Merde.

In certain situations, I'm bilingual.

The fact that I was the only car on the street wasn't my main concern. No. What really had my belly in a free-fall was that this bit of paved real estate was deserted. My last turn had brought me into a long ally bordered by empty warehouses with broken windows and lost dreams. The sinking feeling intensified when a huge tractor-trailer with a ramp attached to the back, loomed ahead.

Actually, the truck itself hadn't given me the lead gut feeling. The big gorilla in a suit with a gun, directing me into the back of said truck, made me realize I was in a bunch of serious doo doo.

I had to stop my car and couldn't back up because my transmission was shot. I hadn't been able to go into reverse for months and kept forgetting to take it in to be fixed. So, I turned off the engine and pocketed the keys.

After my little scare in LA, I'd made the decision I wouldn't willingly go anywhere. I'd also seen enough Oprah to know—don't ever go to the secondary place. Reaching over my left shoulder I locked the door, which gave me a perceived sense of safety. The knuckle dragger could shoot me, but someone would report the gunshot.

Right?

Looking around the area I realized maybe not, but a girl could always hope.

I crouched down a bit lower in an attempt to make myself a smaller target and groped for my purse. Dread washed over me. Instead of my usual knock off designer bag, I still had the tacky hooker purse from LA and didn't have the little gun I usually carried. My only weapon was pepper spray.

Double Merde.

I had less than thirty seconds to think about this because the goon approached my car, and I had to cover my head as he smashed in the driver's window. Then, with apparent ease, he ripped the door off my hatchback.

I gaped in disbelief. This car had been my mother's and I'd inherited it when she died. The Blue Bomb was my last physical link to her and this rusted piece of tin may have been an oil guzzling, exhaust-belching piece of crap, but it was *my* piece of crap.

Jaw clenched, my blood began to boil. Anger might have been out of place, given the circumstances, but I felt no guilt as once again, in less than twenty-four hours, I curled my fingers around the tiny little canister hidden in my purse and waited.

When my attacker turned to come at me through the door, I held my arm out stiff and squeezed. This time mist spewed from the nozzle and hit his face full on. Howling, grabbing at his eyes, he backed away. Not a second to lose, I pretty much fell out of the car, scrambled to my feet, and took off as fast as my still stiff legs would let me.

I found I limbered up pretty quick. Being faced with death will do that for you. I heard him shout and figured he'd be fumbling for his gun, but I wasn't looking back to check. My eyes were on the prize of freedom at the end of the alley. The Olympic record for the one hundred yard dash was about to be broken when I heard bodies collide and a familiar voice cursing behind me.

Tank? What was he doing here?

I skidded to a stop and against my better judgement turned around. Tank and Gorilla Boy fought beside my car. A movement at the front of the truck caught my eye and I spotted a second person jumping down from the big rig.

Now what? I couldn't leave Tank alone with two guys,

he'd be outnumbered. I looked around the alley for a weapon and at first couldn't find anything. Over by a dumpster I spotted a piece of wood about the length of a small baseball bat.

That would work.

Digging the two by four out from under garbage I picked it up and tested its weight in my hand. Good and hefty. It was time to join the fight. The second guy, focused on Tank, didn't even see me approach. Feet spread shoulder width apart I wound up my makeshift bat and cracked him on the back of the head. He dropped like a sack of potatoes, out cold on the pavement. My arms reverberated from the hit.

Ow! Mama Mia... I let go of the two by four and grabbed my hand.

A huge splinter lay lodged in my palm and although I pulled at it with my teeth, the sliver wouldn't budge without making my eyes water. I kicked the second person in the leg, to make sure he was really out cold and not playing possum.

Tank continued to go toe to toe with the big guy. My would-be kidnapper had blood trickling from a cut lip, his breathing labored. Although muscle bound, he wasn't in good shape.

Sometime during the fight the gun had dropped to the ground, so I pounced on it and pointed the barrel at the two men. They continued to punch and grunt, taking no notice of me. I shouted out the only phrase I could think of to make them stop, "Freeze, Police!"

Tank kept going but the massive Neanderthal, caught off guard, paused, which allowed Tank to take advantage of his break in concentration. With a swift upper cut, Tank laid him out flat. Gorilla Boy crumpled to the ground and probably saw little birds tweeting around his head.

Not even breathing heavy Tank looked over his shoulder and grinned. With a dangerous glint in his eye he approached and pulled me against his chest. His head lowered and my lips parted, waiting for a kiss. Instead he whispered in my ear.

"Thanks, Shelby. Now find some rope and tie up the little guy." He slipped the gun from my hand. "I'll take care of Tony here."

"You know him?" How did he know this goon's name and why did I think he'd kiss me?

Tank didn't answer and returned to where Tony lay. I guess I'd find out later, when we had that much needed long talk. I opened the trunk of my car where I kept emergency supplies—a length of rope handily being one of them. It took a few minutes, but I hog-tied the still unconscious man, snagging the splinter several times with the rough rope. The little guy had a cool tattoo on the back of his hand. It was a serpent, inked to look like it was a part of his body, slithering around his bones. Any movement of his hand made the snake 'come to life'.

Tank sat on an overturned crate and kept the gun pointed at our big burly friend while we waited for him to wake up. I watched the entire thing from the side of the Blue Bomb, holding the stick of wood within kicking distance of Tony's partner. When Tony finally came around he didn't look too pleased to see us in control of their roadside diversion. He semi-sat, but went no further when Tank waved the gun at him.

"Anthony. Long time no see. What are you doing in my back yard?"

"I don't got nuthin' to say to youse guys." Tony mumbled.

My eyes rolled heavenward at the classic 'bad guy' line.

Tony obviously didn't have many conversation skills.

"Well Tony, here's how *I* see it. I've got the gun, you don't. This makes me think you'll have a lot to say." Tank scratched his jaw with the barrel of the gun, "Now we can do this easy, or it can go down like our last little meet and greet. You decide."

Tony's eyes, red and irritated from the spray, became huge like saucers. He clearly panicked and blubbered, "Come on man, take it easy. Don't be shooting me again."

Shoot him? Tank shot him?

"Then spill. I'm getting testy and that's my wife you were roughing up."

"Your wife?" Tony paled even more, if that were possible.

Little dude started to wake and, in my humble opinion, move too much, so I gave him a swift kick in the backside, adding a visual reminder by thumping the wooden stick in the palm of my hand. He settled back down with a sullen look on his narrow face.

I'd jammed the sliver deeper and the stupid thing was driving me crazy, so once more I gnawed at my palm, stopping when I heard Tony say, "...so we was to get the girl in the truck and meet up at the warehouse."

That didn't sound too good for me.

"Tony, turn over so I can cuff you and don't even think about running." Tony rolled over and let Tank slap some handcuffs on him. Then Tony struggled back into a sitting position. Tank came over beside my desecrated car and pulled out his phone.

"Yeah, it's me. Tell Neil we have a situation and I need cleaners at..." He looked around. "...the alley at First and Delaware. Bring a flat-bed tow truck." Tank looked down at weasel lying at my feet. He took the two by four from me and propped it against the car.

"Good job." Tank draped an arm around me and squeezed. He flipped the Glock and handed it to me, handle first. "Take this and watch Tony. If he moves, shoot him."

The whole situation was beyond anything I'd ever encountered and I could only stare. I felt like I'd wandered onto a bad movie set and at any moment a skinny, balding man in a beret would jump out from behind a dumpster yelling, "Cut!"

Tank placed both hands on my shoulders, gently turning me to face Tony. With a firm hand he lifted my elbow, so that it was almost shoulder high and away from my body. "Point the gun that way, darlin'."

I racked the slide, popped out the magazine and reloaded the gun. "Thanks. I got it." Tank nodded in appreciation, ducked his head and kissed me quick. The gun laid a little heavy in my hand. My own handgun was a Glock 23 Sub-compact or 'Baby Glock' as others liked to call it. She was pink and I called her '*Baby*'. For me, Baby was the perfect size and when I added the mag extension, she gave me a fantastic grip. Confidence returning, I held the gun on Tony, who looked panic-stricken.

I decided it was payback time and shrugged, levelling a bored look at Tony. "Don't make me use this. I might shoot off something you think is important."

The words hung between us and I heard Tank choke back a laugh. Tony didn't know I was a crack shot. My range instructor called me a freak of nature.

Tank shifted his attention to the smaller man lying on the ground to my right. He'd rolled over onto his back and Tank could now see his face. "Vinnie Malone, what are you doing with Anthony again? Keeping company with him is hazardous to your health."

Vinnie's eyes bulged and sweat poured down his face. Standing near the car, I kept the gun trained on Tony. I wondered again how Tank knew these two guys. My attention pivoted to Tank and Vinnie, but they were talking in low tones.

"…this information does not make me happy Vincent." Tank's voice had risen in anger. "You need to give me a name 'cause when the cleaners get here it won't go good for you, if y'all catch my drift."

I thought Vinnie was going to puke. Fear rolled off him in waves. At least I wanted to think it was fear. I was *not* going to be the one to check if it was something else.

"Aw Tank. I can't. He'd cut off my balls if I ratted."

"Vinnie, he can only cut off what's left after Shelby's shoots 'em." Tank said.

Vinnie turned as grey as the concrete he lay against and looked at me. I waved a salute with the gun. I could almost see the wheels in his brain turning as he weighed his options. Decision made, he took a deep breath and began. "I only talked to this guy on the phone. I never met him. We was to take the girl and her car to this warehouse on Industrial Road. That's all I know. I'm just the driver."

"So, who gave him your names?"

"I don't know, honest."

Tank shook his head. "That's not good business, Vinnie. You should always know who gives your name as referrals. So you can reciprocate." He looked over at Tony. "That means return the favor. Vinnie should always get a name, right Tony?" Tony nodded unenthusiastically, his eyes never leaving the gun.

Tank squatted down beside Vincent, grim-faced. I didn't recognize this man looming over Vinnie. He'd grown bigger, if that was possible and menacing. His face turned hard, like granite and his voice dropped to a deadly whisper. "Vinnie, you could find yourself in a lot of trouble. In fact, you could end up hog-tied in an alley waiting for someone to take you away." He leaned closer. "Take you away somewhere quiet, where no one will hear you. Do you understand what I'm telling you?"

A bead of sweat slowly made its way down the side of Vinnie's face and disappeared under his collar. Visibly shaking, he nodded yes. Tank straightened, but not before he patted Vinnie's cheek, hard. "That's good. We're going to get to the bottom of this."

Just then two nondescript black SUV's pulled into the alley. Four men in matching dark suits and shades piled out followed by a lean, angular man. My first thought was, this is so *Men In Black*. With quiet efficiency they brought Tony and Vincent to their feet and escorted them to the waiting SUVs.

Tank took the Glock from me and brought it to the man I assumed was Neil, who said, "You did it this time, Steele. You blew your cover. I hope she was worth it."

I didn't hear what Tank said, but Neil gave a physical start, then turned and stalked off. I had a strong suspicion Tank hadn't been too polite with the man. Wrong move, if he's your boss.

Throughout all of this, a tow truck backed in and an older male exited, calmly winching the Blue Bomb to the back of the truck. He then threw the door Tony ripped off onto the flat bed portion and I watched him take my car away.

A loud backfire, followed by a series of clunks had me turn and peer down the alley. What was Regis doing here?

"Are you ready to go for a ride?" Startled, I turned to see that Tank had returned and he flashed me a cocky grin. If he was in trouble with Neil, he didn't show it. He threw his arm around my shoulders and steered us toward his motorcycle.

I picked at the splinter again and asked, "Did you see Regis? I heard his car."

"No. Are you sure it was him?"

"Oh yeah. I'd recognize the sound of his old junker anywhere. It's the stuff my nightmares are made of."

That, and being sold into slavery.

Tank shrugged. "Maybe he got side tracked by the detour signs like you. Come on, let's go home."

I checked over my shoulder to see what was happening, but Tank turned my head back and said, "Keep walking. Nothing you'd want to be a witness to."

I shivered and for the first time with Tank's arm around me, not from anticipation.

Chapter Twelve

"Ow, ow, *ow!*"

"Stop being a baby, it's just a splinter."

"No it's not. It's the size of an HB pencil and it hurts."

I sat at the kitchen table while Tank crouched before me and removed the offending sliver of wood with a pair of tweezers. With a satisfied sigh I looked up and found him watching me. Eyes smoldering, lower lip caught between his teeth, he scorched me with that one quick glance. Never taking his eyes off me, he slowly released his lower lip before raising my palm to his mouth.

Oh my.

Heat pooled low in my belly when he pursed his lips and softly blew on the tiny, open wound. The hairs on my arm stood on end and electrical energy shot straight from my hand to the center of my feminine core. Fascinated by his lips, I couldn't take my eyes off them.

He leaned toward me. Would he kiss me? My lips parted in anticipation. Flickers of disappointment stung my pride when all he did was reach around and grab the first-aid kit. He applied some ointment and a Blue Dinosaur Band-Aid. Had I finally pushed him completely away? Utterly embarrassed, I tugged my hand, but he wouldn't let go.

His firm lips pressed above the Band-Aid and I closed my eyes. Kisses feathered the inside of my arm and my breath hitched when he paused at the nape of my neck. The warmth from his body was tangible, the scent of his aftershave and cologne tangy sweet with a hint of musk.

When I opened my eyes, Tank filled my vision. He was a hair's breadth away from my mouth. If I moved even an inch I'd touch his lips with mine. I started to sway forward then caught myself. Tank was not who he said he was, and I needed a lot of answers to a lot of questions.

I scrambled to collect my thoughts as I pushed at his chest. "Slow down, cowboy. We have to talk." I stood and eased around him, toward the kitchen island.

Tank remained in a crouched position for a few seconds longer before rising to his feet. I cut him a glance and noted there was visible evidence he'd also been affected by our closeness. A familiar heat spread beneath my skin. Towering over me, he took up a lot of space in my little kitchen and I was sorely tempted to drag him up to our bedroom. Instead, I busied myself putting away ointment, and Band-Aids and... stuff.

I hesitated when he came up beside me, but instead of hauling me into his arms, he started washing the dishes, which had been left so abruptly this morning. I grabbed a towel and began drying. While we worked in companionable silence, my mind whirred into overtime.

I kept replaying what Neil said. "*You blew your cover. I hope she was worth it.*"

Was cover had he blown, and was I worth it to him?

As I put away the last dish, I heard the fridge door open and turned to see him holding a beer. He grabbed a second bottle, silently asking me if I wanted one. I nodded and took it from him. Drink in hand, I followed him to the living room where I curled in the big easy chair and waited while he paced.

He took a long draw from his beer, pushed a hand through his hair and rubbed the back of his neck. The last time I'd seen him this jumpy was right before he met my family. Finally he stopped pacing and faced me.

"You've obviously figured out I'm not a PI." He chuckled when he saw me roll my eyes.

"Duh!"

"I can't give you a lot of details, I work for NSU." He must have caught my puzzled look. "Name's not important. It's a small agency within a larger government branch. They recruited me right out of the military. Three years ago I came here on a job with my buddy Caleb and ran into Ben Grady. We'd all gone through basic together."

He finished his beer and set the empty bottle on the coffee table. "Ben's the one who insisted we go to the beach party where I met you. You kinda fell into my arms and I couldn't let go."

At this beach party, Regis once again stalked me. When I'd gone to leave, as in run screaming, I'd stumbled into a solid wall. The wall turned out to be Tank, my knight in tattered jeans. Panicked, I begged him to pretend he was my boyfriend. What started as a ploy to get rid of Regis, ended up as reality.

"When that job was done I requested to stay here and make this my home base. The PI thing was an excellent cover. It gave me an excuse to ask a lot of questions and not stick out in the crowd. So they set me up with a legitimate business and let us go to it."

That explained all the business trips, without me. The business trips I'd been convinced were for Tank to meet someone else. "You could have told me. I would have understood."

"No, darlin', I couldn't."

I finally voiced the fear which burned in me. "Did you leave me for another woman?"

Did I even want to hear the answer?

Tank sat on the coffee table and leaned toward me. "No. I didn't. When I left and made you believe there was someone else... it cut my heart out. We have an agent, who's been deep undercover in a crime syndicate for over seven years. The operative got wind my activities had spooked one paranoid pain in the butt, so I had to disappear for a while. If Carlos had become serious about checking me out, he'd have found you. Making it look like we split was the only way I knew to keep you safe."

Tank was a good actor. He'd fooled me and everyone I knew.

"Well... It so happens that my *'problem'* met a...premature death in New York." Tank chuckled at my reaction. "Not by me. He apparently was making some extra bucks his boss didn't know about and that was okay. But he was using the extra dough to buy gifts and trinkets for the boss's mistress and that's not okay."

Tank reached out and took hold of my hand, kissing the Band-Aid on my palm and then each finger individually. Between each sizzling kiss, while I melted into a gooey puddle, he spoke slow and soft. "I'm back for good."

Thirty thousand questions scrambled around my brain and it didn't help that all my girly parts were waking up with his kisses. As much as I wanted—no—needed Tank to hold me tight and let nature take its natural course, we had to square away everything that happened the last few days.

I needed answers, not sex. *Liar*, my libido growled, I needed both.

I pulled my fingers from his warm grip, snatched up the empty beer bottles and carried them into the kitchen. I turned to go back to the living room and ran into the solid wall of his chest.

Déjà vu, just like when I met him the first time on the beach.

Big hands reached out and steadied me. My palms slid across his muscled torso on their own accord. It would be so easy to stand on tiptoe, kiss him and forget all the questions racing around my hormone driven mind. Sweep them under a rug and look at them later.

I lifted my hands off his forearms. No. We were going to finish this talk and I had to keep a clear head. Stepping back a pace, I leaned with my back against the kitchen island. He gave me a look that promised more, but wisely, Tank slid around to sit on a stool at the island and waited.

I rubbed my forehead, thinking about what Tank had shared. He hadn't left me for another woman, but he also hadn't trusted me enough to be honest and tell me the whole truth. It was as if I were a ribbon twisting with each new puff of air. If it was safe for Tank to come back to me why did someone try to kidnap me? I asked him that very question.

"I'm not sure. I think it has more to do with Harrison." He answered.

"Harrison? Is he part of the crime syndicate?"

"No, Harrison got in *way* over his head with someone we've come to refer to as the 'Big Boss.' He tried to use his daddy's influence to squeeze out of it, but Big Boss wouldn't let him go. I've been in contact with Harry for a couple of months now and we finally got everything in place so he could turn states evidence against this elusive piece of dirt."

While Tank spoke, I began fitting the pieces together in my mind. But my puzzle still had gaping holes in it.

"How did I get involved in all this? You told me he was a suspect in a murder."

"I know. We figured Harry's phone was tapped, so we had him call his parents weekly and talk about Lulu. Through Dango, my buddy with the LAPD, whom you met just recently"—I rolled my eyes— "we created a cover story of Harrison getting friendly with a call girl and going AWOL when he was implicated in the murder. To make his disappearance look and feel legit we had Raymond call you to report him missing. We actually have Harry stashed away in a motel."

That explained the strange vibes I'd gotten from the Grants. It had all been an act. I knew it!

Tank continued. "That way when I showed up to nose around it wouldn't look suspicious, given our history."

While I digested this information, I replayed everything that had transpired over the past couple of days. "I went to LA, searched Harrison's condo and it was all for nothing...the hooker outfit...the call girls—" I stopped midsentence. "The call girls. I talked to some hookers. They knew Lulu and Harry. How can that be?"

"I overheard you tell Polly you were going to find some hookers, so I had to rustle up some 'girls' for you to talk to. I owe huge favors to a couple of our female agents. The cars driving by were other agents making sure you believed them." He pushed to his feet and paced like a caged animal. "I don't know why I haven't heard anything yet."

My eyes widened as a realization hit me. "If I intercepted a coded confirmation would I understand the message?"

He stopped pacing. "Probably not. Why?"

"Well, this morning, while you were in the shower, I answered your phone by mistake. The message was, *enter a four digit code from your computer* or something like that. I forgot to tell you in all the excitement."

He looked grim as he pulled out his laptop and placed it on the kitchen table. He waited, impatiently tapping the sides as it booted up. I watched as he opened file after file, entering codes and scanning information as it flashed across the screen. He pulled out his phone and entered some numbers, then went back to his laptop. Fixated on the various emotions crossing his face, I knew exactly when he reached the 'ah ha' moment.

Then his brow furrowed again.

"What's wrong?" I asked.

His gaze remained vacant for a long moment and then he smiled. I knew in my bones he did that to reassure me. He shut the computer down and asked, "Do you want pizza?"

"Pizza?" I stammered.

"Yeah, I'm starved." Tank grabbed his jacket and threw it on. Shoving his laptop back into his leather saddlebag, he tossed the strap over his shoulder and headed down the hall to the front door.

One minute we're talking about spies, secret information, undercover operatives and he wants to go for pizza?

He called out. "I'll be back in about thirty minutes, forty-five tops. Do you want everything on it?"

From the kitchen I yelled back, "Yes, no, wait... No anchovies." I hated anchovies. Too salty and they made me bloat. I heard Tank roar off on his motorcycle and idly wondered how he'd carry the pizza home. I started to put the empty beer bottles in the recycling bin, then stopped abruptly.

He wasn't going for pizza. He was going to meet someone.

Geez, Tank. When will you trust me?

I grabbed the keys and ran out to my car but the empty

driveway reminded me that I didn't have a car anymore. It had been towed. Stomping my foot in frustration I watched the tail lights of his bike turn the corner.

He'd be miles away before I could get Aunt Tillie's 1964 Austen-Healy Sprite started. Shoving the keys into my pocket I turned to go back into the house. Tank better have a good explanation when he got home. A glint in the waning sunlight caught my attention. I paused when I saw, to my left, what looked like a copper wire snaking across my driveway leading into the neighbor's shrubbery.

I don't know what happened first, the deafening sound or the sudden force of wind that threw me to the ground. Immense heat seared my neck and arms and a piercing, sharp pain slammed near my temple.

Everything went black.

Chapter Thirteen

Tank rumbled down the quiet street and brought his motorcycle to a stop near 105 LaRue. He kicked out the stand and locked his bike. Not that it would do much good in this neighborhood. Shrugging the collar of his leather jacket up, he started walking toward a run-down section of tenement houses and buildings.

Late afternoon sunlight struggled to reach the asphalt, cutting a narrow ribbon through abandoned cars, strewn garbage and dilapidated, forgotten billboards. Faded curtains twitched in a murky window; the only sign of life. After a few minutes the acrid stench of garbage no longer burned the back of his throat, but his eyes still watered.

He thought back on Shelby's attempted abduction and subsequent series of events that led to him revealing what he did for a living. A dead weight settled in his stomach when he thought about what could have happened if he hadn't followed her this morning. If he'd have been even ten minutes later he probably never would have seen her again. He couldn't imagine life without her. Even when she was mad, he loved being around her.

Sometimes he preferred her spittin' mad. Kinda kept things interesting.

He remembered the dazed look on Tony's face when Shelby stood over him like an avenging angel, holding a gun that was too big for her hand and a wry smile tugged at his mouth. She handled it like a pro. That was his girl.

He *should* be back at their place cozying up with her, trying to steal a few more kisses. Instead he was in this flea infested area meeting Rodie, one of the best undercover operatives the agency had.

Rodie left an urgent message in an encrypted e-mail to meet him behind 105 LaRue at eighteen hundred hours. Tank was uneasy. Everything about this stank, much like the neighborhood. In the seven years he'd worked with him, Rodie contacted him twice outside their arranged meetings. And both times had been nothing but bad news.

Tank itched in his don't-wanna-itch-place, again.

The alleyway behind the row of neglected warehouses had two exits. He entered the one furthest away from 105 LaRue in order to get a lay of the land. He'd learned in Afghanistan to be cautious. A quick look at the roofline assured him no one was set up to sniper, although anyone could be hiding behind the dumpsters and recycling bins that littered the alley.

A scraping sound ahead made him pause. He eased around the corner, checking for the source and stopped cold at the sight of a woman, her back to him. Her curly black hair was pulled away from her face and poked through a bright red baseball cap. She was watching the other exit. He continued to slide closer when movement in his peripheral vision had him reach for her shoulder, instinctively moving her out of danger.

He found himself looking at the barrel of a gun, pointed straight at his heart. Ice blue eyes assessed him from under the cap. Hands held away from his body, Tank backed up a step.

"You're late." She lowered the gun, tucking it back into

a discreet holder clipped to her belt. He lowered his hands, but remained wary, not knowing if she was friend or foe. Probably friend, as she hadn't shot him. That was always a good sign.

He checked the alley to see what spooked him and decided it must been a rat. Today's activities had him a little on edge. The woman crossed her arms and leaned back on one hip, looking him over from top to bottom and then all the way back.

"So, you're the famous Agent Jake Steele. Or should I call you Tank?"

Years of training kept his stance natural. How did she know who he was?

"Who—"

"Rodie told me."

What was Rodie up to now?

"How'd you know Rodie?" Tank's brain kicked into overdrive. Why wasn't Rodie here? Was this a set up?

"Met him through Charlie and Slash."

That would have to be One Eyed Charlie and J.D. 'Slash 'em, Stash 'em' Rogers. She was rattling off his contacts like she had his smart phone in front of her.

"Look... Whoever you are...."

"Liz."

"Alright, *Liz*. I don't know who you are, or how you know my, uh... friends, but I'm supposed to be meeting one of them here and they won't show if I've got company. *Comprende*?"

Tank heard her chuckle. She actually chuckled.

"Rodie told me you'd be tough. Why do you think I'm here? For my health?" Liz fished out a wallet and showed him her badge and identification card. She hailed from Washington. The uneasy feeling in his gut intensified.

"Head office sent me. Rodie's gone so deep he'll need a diver's suit. But, he managed to get two messages out. One to you, to meet here and one to me, to give you a head's up." She flipped the wallet shut and stuck it into her back pocket.

His eyes narrowed at the last phrase. Heads up, for what? "I'm not a happy camper, Liz. You need to talk to me or I'm turning around, getting on my bike and going home to my wife." He swung on his heel and headed back down the alley. Her hand on his forearm stopped him.

"Don't you mean *ex*-wife?"

"We're working things out." He tried to shrug out of her grip but she tightened her grip.

"There's been a hit put out on you."

He froze and looked back over his shoulder. "What do you mean a *hit*?"

She let go of his arm. "Exactly what I said. A hit. Your cover's been blown on the Grant case and Rodie said a contract's been drawn up."

"The timing's all wrong. Rodie sent me the message last night, before my cover was blown. How could they know to put out a hit?"

"We think today's fun and games were to draw you into the open. Confirm what Big Boss knew, or thought he did. You gotta hit the ground running and get out of here. We've got a 'copter waiting. Is there anything you need back at the house?"

Tank started to say *No*, then realization hit him like a power-packed punch to the gut. He ran for his motorcycle.

Footsteps pounded as Liz raced behind him, "Steele! Where are you going?"

He hopped on his bike and unlocked it; cold sweat poured down his back. His lips curled into a feral snarl, "Shelby's back at the house, unprotected."

He didn't wait for a response. He throttled the bike and roared off at top speed, toward their house. An agonizing ten minutes passed before he skidded around the final corner and screeched to a halt. Immediately he was aware of fire-trucks, police cars and finally, a medical examiner's car.

Black.

Solitary.

Death itself parked at the end of his driveway.

Fire fighters had the flames under control and police were busy keeping spectators from crossing the temporary yellow-taped lines encircling the yard. He was vaguely aware of a car purring to a stop behind him. Then he felt a hand on his arm.

Her soft voice filtered through the cold numbness. "Steele. You gotta get out of here. We'll find out what's going on. Come on."

Anger, fast and swift, coursed through him. He shrugged off her hand. "Look, Liz. I don't give a rat's ass if everybody knows who I am. Get out of my way."

He headed in the direction of the chaos. A police officer stopped him when he approached the yellow-taped barrier. "I'm sorry, sir, this is off limits to the public. You'll have to step away."

Tank reached into his back pocket and pulled out his wallet. He flashed his badge in the officer's face. "Agent Steele, NSU."

The young officer allowed him to pass, but the look on his face let Tank know that whatever he'd find, it wasn't going to be good. As he walked across the lawn Tank formulated a plan to get as much information as he could before the authorities realized who he was and cornered him in some room for questioning.

Tank ran an experienced eye over the house. The first

floor looked like it had heavy damage, the second floor untouched. Damage was concentrated around the front door and porch. All the windows at the front of the house had been blown inside.

Crossing the lawn, he approached what looked like one of the investigators. A short, balding man watched him. Tank flashed his badge again. Never missing a beat the man drawled, "Didn't take long for the big boys to come and play in our sandbox." He crushed out a cigarette with the toe of his shoe. "I'm Lieutenant DeMarco and that's—" nodding over to a tall, skinny, red haired man, "—my partner, Detective Rawlins."

Tamping down his fear, Tank asked, "So, what've you got?" He wouldn't look at the medical examiner's car.

"What we *got* is a blown up house. Whoever set the charges wanted to make sure there was a lot of noise and smoke." He extracted his duty book and scanned the few notes he'd already started.

"Any casualties?" Nausea racked Tank's body.

DeMarco nodded his head at the coroner's vehicle, which was slowly pulling away and read from his notes. "Yeah. Female, mid-twenties. A passer-by found her on the driveway. Never knew what hit her..."

Tank didn't hear any more. He sprinted toward the Medical Examiner's car and banged on the driver's window. Startled, the Coroner slammed on the brakes. The whir of the window sliding down was followed by a tired sigh from the man seated behind the wheel.

"Yes?" The Coroner glanced in his rear-view mirror. Tank figured he was checking to make sure the gurney holding Shelby's body hadn't tipped over when he hit the brakes.

"I'm her husband. Could I...? Could I see her before

you take her away?"

"I don't think that's a good idea, son." The kind face of the Coroner caused Tank's control to slip a little further. The doctor put the car in gear.

Tank gripped the man's shoulder. The doctor braked again and looked up at Tank.

"Wait. You don't understand. I *need* to see her." Tank released his hold when the coroner shifted and winced. "Please."

Eternity passed before the doctor slid the car into park. Tank stepped aside as he opened the car door and shuffled around to the back of the vehicle. The Coroner grabbed the door and swung it wide, reached in and pulled out the gurney Shelby's body was strapped to. He untied a few ropes and gently peeled back the blanket covering her face.

Tank's heart stopped beating for a few seconds and then thudded back to life. She was so still, he could almost believe she was only sleeping. Her hair curled about her shoulders and her lashes looked like dark smudges against ashen cheeks. He reached out a trembling hand and brushed the errant curl that was forever getting in her eyes and tucked it behind her ear. It was then he noticed the bloody trail that ran from her temple, down the side of her face, onto her neck. *You can't be dead.* He caressed her cheek with the back of his finger.

Oh God! She was still warm!

He'd been this close to saving her. Anguish ripped through him and he almost doubled over, his breath catching in his throat.

"Are you okay, son?" The Coroner replaced the blanket and pushed the gurney back into the car.

Unable to speak, Tank nodded his reply and watched as the man climbed back into the car and drove off with his wife into the dark night.

He turned and walked away, back toward his bike and Liz, waiting in the shadows. As he passed where she stood, concealed in the dark, he bit out, "I want who did this dead. Pull Rodie out if you have to, I want them dead."

Chapter Fourteen

Crisp air, daffodils and tulips struggled to push through the ground. Tank sat at Shelby's gravesite with Polly clutching his hand, sobbing quietly. As she dabbed a tissue to her red rimmed eyes, he looked around at the few friends of Shelby's who'd gathered.

He caught a glimpse of Regis, lurking behind a tall cedar.

Polly followed his line of sight and sniffled. "Who's he gonna haunt now that Shelby's gone?" They both watched Regis slink back to his beaten up truck, and drive off with a loud back-firing bang.

The casket began its slow descent and his stomach clenched. Tank stood, refusing to watch his only love leave the sunlight forever. He wished he could stay and offer comfort to Polly, but he couldn't. This wound was too raw, too deep to focus on any reminders of Shelby.

Polly glanced up, understanding on her face. She reached out and touched his arm, but he turned away. The two women had been inseparable for so long, he couldn't look at her without seeing Shelby.

The solitary walk back to his motorcycle was interminable. He swung his leg over the seat and for a moment, his attention was caught by the sight of a plump robin, head cocked to one side, waiting for the worm to make one wrong move in the ground. Shelby loved the red breasted bird. She'd often said her first child would be called Robin, boy or girl.

He ruthlessly cut the thought off. There would be no children, no tomorrows for him and Shelby. There was nothing.

He roared off to a motel and changed. Bundling the suit he'd bought for the funeral into a large ball, he stuffed it into a bag, and dropped it off at a clothing collection depot. He needed no reminders of today. He drove for hours before exhaustion forced him to find a motel by the side of the road. Before registering, he stopped at an all-night liquor store.

He'd just unlocked his motel room when a familiar ring tone emanated from his jacket pocket. Irritated for not turning his phone off, he hesitated, unconsciously squaring his shoulders before answering.

"Mother."

"Montgomery, you know how much I dislike your monosyllabic greetings."

"Yes, and you know I don't answer to Montgomery. My name is Jake."

"There's no need to be so confrontational. I've been trying to get a hold of you for days. I'd heard that girl you lived with has died. Are you okay?"

"She was my wife, mother. My wife, not some 'girl' I lived with." Tank forced his response through stiff lips.

His parents never met Shelby. Whether by accident or design, Tank never knew. No one in their eyes was good enough for Montgomery Jackson III, a persona and lifestyle he'd shed a lifetime ago.

"Mont— Jake, please." Her voice pleaded over the phone. "Come home, son. We need you. Your father needs you."

It took all his energy to keep his voice civil and not yell at his mother, who never even tried to get to know the woman he loved. To find out what her favorite color was, or what made Shelby laugh so hard she'd fall back into her chair and almost tip it over.

"You mean the business needs me."

"Yes it does, but that's not why I called. We..." She sighed deeply. "I miss you. Please come home."

"I can't and I won't."

He turned off his phone and entered the motel room with a bottle of Jack Daniels in his hand. The heir to Jackson Steele, worth a few billion dollars, intended to get stinking drunk.

****

Tank leaned back onto the bar with his elbows and surveyed the room. Smoke hung in the air, creating a hazy fog and he could barely see to the other side over crowds of people. Music twanged out of a jukebox and a young couple swayed on the tiny space carved out between close set tables, oblivious to everyone around them.

Don't they all look just freaking happy? Here's to your continued happiness.

He went to toast the dancing couples with his drink and realized the glass was empty. Turning slightly to his right, he placed the empty on the bar and called out to the bartender.

"Yo, buddy. One more."

The bartender, drawing a mug of ale glanced at him. "I don't think so. You've had enough."

Tank straightened and turned fully around. "I *said* I wanted another."

"Look, *buddy*. Y'all had enough."

Over Tank's shoulder the bartender signaled the

bouncers. Grinning, Tank rolled his shoulders. Finally he could get rid of a little frustration and have some fun.

Alright. Let's see if these boys are ready to rumble.

He turned and looked directly into the chest of what had to be the largest man Tank had ever seen in his life. Which was pretty large. Tank knew he stood six foot, five inches in bare feet. His line of sight rose to a big smile, minus one or two teeth.

Hesitation had him stall for a second, then he thought, "*Got nuthin' to lose,*" and drew back his fist. Time slowed down and in that small bit of eternity he saw his clenched hand connect with the giant's palm and then a sledge hammer disguised as a beefy fist hit him square between the eyes. His next solid memory was being tossed through the door, onto the parking lot gravel.

"Don't come back, if you know what's good fer ya."

Face and hands scraped, Tank lay there gasping, trying to catch his breath. The bouncer must have hit him in the solar plexus as well. He stopped trying to push up and flopped back down.

He was so tired, so very, very tired. A woman's soft voice cut through his drunken haze. It sounded as though she was right in his face. "Geez, Steele, your breath would peel wallpaper."

Small hands wedged beneath his chest and tried to roll him over.

"Man, you weigh a ton," she grunted, still trying to move him.

She was starting to tick him off. He pried one bloodshot eye open and growled, "Go 'way. Lemme sleep."

"Oh no, sunshine. We need to get you into a motel and sober you up. I'm tired of watching you drink yourself into the grave you so obviously desire."

Tank pushed himself onto his side and caught the woman around the waist, pulling her so that she fell on top of him. He cupped her bottom and held her, rocking his hips, pushing into her natural cradle. It felt so good to be holding Shelby again.

"Desire? You wanna feel my obvious desire?" He bumped up his hips and the woman gasped.

She struggled to free herself, all the while cursing. "Let me go, you drunk Neanderthal. What is it with guys? You only think with one thing."

She managed to free herself from his arms, but as she pushed off, he grabbed her hand and held tight. He couldn't lose her again. He brought her hand to his lips and pressed a kiss to her palm. "Shelby?"

He couldn't keep his eyes open. All he wanted to do was go to sleep and never wakeup. She tugged her hand from him and whispered. "You sure loved her, didn't you."

With startling clarity Tank realized it wasn't Shelby in the parking lot with him, but Liz. As he sank back into drunken oblivion he heard her say. "He's in pretty rough shape. Get Rodie over here."

****

Bright lights hurt his eyes and Tank brought his hand up to shade them. Squinting, he noticed the curtains in the room drawn wide, the window cracked open. He groped around for a bottle, which should have been beside the bed on the floor. There was nothing there.

Propping himself onto his elbow, he leaned over to look for one. The room swam into focus and he saw it was tidy and smelled clean. His clothes lay draped over a chair and he was under the blankets in his underwear. He didn't remember putting on underwear.

Shoot, he didn't remember taking off his clothes. Balancing on his hands, he got his bearings before nature's call forced him to get up and shuffle into the bathroom.

He stood facing the toilet and, left arm braced against the wall, aimed for the bowl.

"Well, well. You're finally awake," a voice drawled from the door.

Tank looked under his supporting arm, acknowledging a thin, dark haired man leaning against the doorjamb, a slick smirk on his face. He flushed the toilet, washed his hands, dried them on a pristine white towel and then drove his fist into the man's face, dropping him to the floor. Stepping over the prone body, Tank stalked over to his clothes and started dragging them on.

He cast a glance back at the man, who'd raised himself to his feet and now rubbed his reddened jaw. Tank waited to feel any remorse. Nope, nothing.

"What do you want, Rodie?" His anger simmered. Why hadn't Rodie gotten Shelby out of the house before anything happened?

Rodie sat on the edge of the bed, keeping a wary eye on Tank. "Is this how you say hello to old friends?"

Tank launched himself from the chair and grabbed Rodie by the shirt collar, dragging him up so that Rodie's face was inches from his own. "*Are* you my friend?" Tank sneered. "What happened? Start talkin' or I'll drop you again. And this time I won't be nice about it."

Rodie squirmed and pushed. "Hey man, don't get testy with me. I tried to get your sorry backside out before things went down."

Tank released his grip, letting Rodie fall back onto the bed. "Yeah, remind me to thank you, when I care."

Going over to his jacket, hanging by the door, Tank

reached into a pocket. He brought out a gun, checked the magazine and satisfied it was loaded, tucked it into the back waistband of his jeans. Shrugging into his jacket, he faced Rodie.

"Look, I get that you lost your old lady." Rodie ran his fingers through his hair, causing the ends to stand straight up. "I know how much she meant to you, more than anybody. But you gotta move on, man. Harrison's been giving us more details than a horny cheerleader's diary ever since Vinnie was iced—"

"Vinnie Malone?"

"Yup. One and the same. After the botched kidnap attempt he was found in the back of a movie theatre, throat slit wide open. Kind of ironic when you think about it."

Tank paused putting on his boots. "Why?"

"The movie playing was *The Godfather*." Rodie chuckled softly, rolling a coin between his fingers absentmindedly.

Tank had finished dressing, but stayed seated in the chair beside the nicked wooden table. He registered the name of the motel on the stationery. It looked like he was in Arkansas. He hated Arkansas.

Rodie continued, "It's time to get back into the game, man."

"Don't you get it Rodie? I don't care anymore."

Rodie stood and paced with quick, nervous steps. "You should care. Big Boss needs to be brought down. I've spent seven years undercover ferreting this jerk out and you need retribution, man."

"What I need is for you to get out of my sight."

"Nah, that's too easy, man. Look, Big Boss put the hit on you, not the girl. This was personal, taking out your girl this way. It's gotta be someone who knows you."

Tank inhaled sharply at the forced memory of Shelby's house. The fire blackened front door and window. How the glass and wood had blown into the house, destroying the hall entrance.

He sat ramrod straight.

Blown *into* the house? *Think, Steele!*

Rodie walked to the window and through a crack in the curtains, looked outside. A habit most field agents couldn't lose, no matter where they were. A glimmer of an idea took shape as Tank watched Rodie pace.

"Rodie?"

Rodie stopped and looked over. His eyes shifted to the window, then back to Tank. "What?"

Tank leaned back in the chair, stretched his legs out and crossed them at the ankles. "What does it mean to you, the explosion blowing everything *into* the house?"

Rodie scratched his head as he pondered the question. "I guess it means the charges were light, laid maybe at the base of the windows. I've seen photos. Damage was not that bad once all the smoke cleared. It looked a lot worse than it actually was."

Tank ran a hand over his chin. He needed a shave. "I agree. It had to be someone in the area who knew when we'd be there."

He'd shoved the memories of that night down deep and hadn't allowed them any air to breath, but now he brought them out, recalling all the details with heart sickening precision. There hadn't been any suspicious vehicles or any strangers on the street. Shelby's corner of the world had been a nice quiet area with neighbors who'd lived there for years. Everybody knew everybody. Regis was the only person around Shelby's house the night before the explosion. Tank recalled Shelby's aversion to him, and without realizing it, said his name aloud.

"Did you say Regis?" Rodie perked up. "That's interesting."

Tank waved his hand dismissively. "I'm just thinking out loud. He's Shelby's neighbor and he was there the night before the explosion, but he's a mama's boy. He couldn't find his way down a straight tunnel, even with GPS and directions."

"Hold on a minute. That name came up a few times when we were talking to Harrison. We brushed it off because Harrison seems to think he's just a peripheral player. Maybe he was trying to impress the boss by taking you out, but got the girl instead. He'd blend in, no one would notice him if he 'scoped out the place."

Tank remembered seeing Regis come from around the side of Shelby's house when she'd returned from LA, not from the sidewalk. He'd noticed him as he parked his bike on the street. At the time he thought the weasel only wanted to ask her out again, but now he sensed something deeper, more sinister.

Then he recalled the offhand comment Regis made, *I thought you were in LA.*

He'd been so stupid. Or blind. How could he have missed the signs? Tank's voice was deadly cold when he said to Rodie. "Call Neil. I want a surveillance team on Regis."

****

Feet kicked out over the porch railing, Tank sipped a beer and watched agency vehicles and swarms of forensic teams arrive, only to disappear into Regis' house. Tank appeared calm, almost nonchalant, but he raged on the inside.

Surveillance confirmed Regis was involved with Big Boss and had set the charges at Shelby's house. Tank's first impulse had been to drag the simpering worm out of his house and take him to a secluded, quiet place where he would do things. Things that took time.

He daydreamed about it, relishing the idea of the pain and fear Regis would experience, but the burning anger dissipated and Tank decided revenge was best served by letting Regis sweat it out in prison. Tank would let it slip, when they interviewed Regis that a few of the bigger men behind the cold silent walls were looking for dates. Regis had a vivid imagination. Let him figure it out.

His cell phone vibrated. Reaching into his back pocket he pulled the phone out and checked caller ID. His tight voice betrayed the tension coiling in the back of his neck. "Steele."

"The little ferret's been under our noses the whole time." Rodie's excited voice shot through the phone. "It appears he was more involved with Big Boss than we thought. Regis did a lot of business for him, using gadgets on the phone to disguise his voice—"

"Have you got him in custody?" Tank asked.

"Yeah and you should see his basement, man. Freaking space age."

"I'll be there in two." Tank turned off his phone, set the empty beer bottle on the porch, and walked down the street. How convenient Regis lived only three houses away. The irony was not lost on him.

****

The interior of the house bustled with activity and Tank, pushing by some agents searching a closet, made his way to the basement. With one sweeping glance he saw Regis had set up an intricate computer lab on the right and the left side of the basement housed bankers boxes stacked five high and he couldn't tell how many deep. The room felt cold, almost sterile, smelling of bleach and chlorine.

Regis had been meticulous with his record keeping and surveillance of Big Boss's 'troops.' Tank looked over the shoulder of the computer forensic analyst, watching column after column of numbers scroll down one of three screens, set up on a steel tube desk.

"What do you have?" Tank thought his eyes would cross. There were a lot of dates, names and numbers.

"What don't we have would be a better question. Regis tried to clean his computer before we got here, but I've been able to reconstruct most of it." The analyst took off his glasses and rubbed the bridge of his nose. He indicated the screen on the left. "This file is drug deals. Who bought, who sold. See the ones in red?"

Tank leaned in and saw a few names highlighted in red.

"We think these are ones who didn't pay."

"What makes you say that?"

"Red is dead." The analyst scrolled the page back up a few screens and the cursor hovered over a name, Dino PasQuale. "See Dino here?"

"Yeah, wasn't he found floating a few years ago?'

"Yup, that's him and right about the time Dino was killed, you'll see Angelo's name in the payment column."

Tank nodded. That made sense. It was a well-known fact that Dino's brother Angelo had continued the business. "What else have you got?"

"Lots. This egg head kept everything. This one..." A few clicks and another file popped up on the second screen. "...itemizes robberies in the area and a few out of state. He lists who Big Boss hired, who got what percentage of the take. He even rated them on a sliding scale. It's like hitting a gold mine. We've been able to get some warrants out on a few people, all because our little buddy is an anal idiot. Too bad a lot of the trails are dead ends with closed numbered accounts, but we're working every angle we've got to find the identity of Big Boss."

"Agent Steele?" Tank turned to see another agent, hesitating at the foot of the stairs. "I think you should see this."

Tank followed him to the second floor, toward the master bedroom. He stopped cold in the doorway and took a deep breath, forcing himself to enter and take a closer look. His hands clenched and he shook with an almost uncontrollable anger.

The illegal business Regis was involved in, Tank could understand, but what he saw in this room kicked him in the gut. The far wall was covered in a collage of photos taken of Shelby, proving Regis had stalked her for years.

There were photos of her at work, talking on the phone in her kitchen even sunbathing in her back yard. But the one that almost had Tank drop to his knees was of him and Shelby, taken through a window. He recognized the dress she was wearing. He'd just proposed, and she'd said yes. Closing his eyes, he still smelled her perfume.

The picture forever encapsulated them in a passionate embrace, his one hand cupping her face, the other pulling her close to his body. Her arms were wound around his neck with her fingers tangled in his hair. He'd been kissing her passionately, deeply and so in love, and he hated Regis for taking her away before he could explain that he never stopped loving her.

The agent finished snapping photos of the scene and removed that same picture off the wall, and began to place it into an evidence pouch. Tank snatched the photo out of his hand. The agent, taken by surprise, reached for the picture. "Sir, that's evidence."

"This one stays with me. She's more than a manila folder full of photos." Tank's voice brooked no argument and the agent, after a slight pause nodded, moving over to other pictures on the wall. Tank carefully tucked the photo into his wallet and turned his back on the abhorrent shrine.

Sue Barr

Chapter Fifteen

Everything hurt.

I tried turning my head side to side. My stomach rolled with nausea, but not enough to throw up. Nothing seemed familiar as I looked around a spacious room with pale yellow walls. Bright blue curtains framed a large, oversized window and I could tell dusk approached. The double bed I lay in was comfortable enough and a quick check under the patterned quilt showed I wore a lacy, white cotton nightgown. Did I even own a nightgown and where was I?

I raised myself to a sitting position and my stomach lurched again, but quickly settled. On the far side of the room opposite the bed, I saw an adjoining bathroom. Relief rolled over me. Nature called and the last thing I wanted was to try and stumble down some hallway.

With cautious movements I swung my legs over the edge of the bed and stood. Kneecaps shaking, I began to cross the room when dizziness hit me full force. Edges of black crept in around my vision and I had to prop my weight on the bed with one arm.

Head lowered, to staunch the feeling of nausea that had returned with a vengeance, I heard the door creak open. Feeling like a naughty child caught out of bed I froze, my gaze raised to a tall, lean stranger standing in the doorway.

He rushed to my side and wrapped a strong arm around

my waist, giving me the support I needed. "Wait a minute. I'll help you," he said, "Where were you going?"

"Bathroom. *NOW*!" Urgent need crowded out time for niceties and small talk. I didn't even mind that a complete stranger was going to help me.

"Then we better hustle. I'll get you there and give you some privacy."

He helped me to the bathroom and then eased back out, closing the door. I waited until I knew for certain he'd moved away before I sat to attend my needs.

The smallest of tasks almost proved too much for me. I stood to wash my hands and the room dipped and swayed. Only by hanging onto the counter did I stop myself from falling.

In the mirror, a stranger's bright blue eyes stared back at me. A sterile gauze strip at my temple blended in with the pasty white of my forehead. There was also gauze on the side of my neck and a few bruises on my shoulder peeked out from under the collar of the nightgown. No shadow of recognition hit me.

I must have made a noise because after a light tap, the door opened and he popped his head in again.

"You okay? Do you need a hand getting back to bed?"

Weakly, I nodded.

"Don't mind me." He scooped me up, easily carrying me back into the bedroom. With gentle care I was laid onto the bed and then the stranger pulled the duvet to cover me again.

He dragged a chair from under the window to the side of the bed, sat on it and leaned forward until his forearms rested on his thighs. He had thick, wavy, chestnut hair, chocolate brown eyes and a rugged face.

I wished he had hair the color of burnished oak, tipped

with golden highlights and green eyes, or did I like blue? He looked at me with a concerned expression. My eyelids drooped and I struggled to keep them open.

"Who are you?" I finally asked.

"I'm…a friend." The pause made my brow furrow. That was not an honest answer. How did I know that?

My last coherent thought, before I fell back asleep was, "Who am I?"

****

Before I knew it a week had passed. Caleb, that was the stranger's name, helped me with most things and brought me meals. Conversation never strayed into personal areas. In fact, Caleb didn't talk much at all. Although he told me my name was Dixie.

As my strength returned I began sitting on the window seat in my bedroom, looking outside. The mountains in the distance created a slate blue border for the valley spread below the house, which rested on a remote ridge.

Sunsets were my favorite time of day. When the sun began to disappear behind the line of mountains, tinges of red and orange were flung into the sky, changing to a purple so deep it seemed almost blue. Darkness would settle, gather in the hollow of the valley and then climb, overtaking our ridge. Something that beautiful should have been memorable, but it wasn't.

After another week the bandages came off my neck and arms. A gentle, country doctor visited to remove stitches and checked the burns on the back of my hands and neck. Fortunately they were minor and healed with very little scarring. Well, not any physical scarring that is. Frustration became my best friend as I struggled to kick-start my memory bank.

I hounded Caleb to bring me books and told myself fairy tales, thinking I could trick my mind into letting something slip. But it stayed tighter than a snare drum.

After the doctor's visit, I was brushing my teeth and looked at my reflection. Some of my hair had been shaved in a little patch at my temple, the rest of it bounced around my shoulders in springy curls. A thought popped into my head, like a picture. I saw myself with curls tumbling down my back. This happened a lot. Bits of my memory would flash in and then go. If I tried to capture them, to make them stay so I could study them, I'd get a terrible headache.

Caleb came upstairs and stopped at the open door to my room. A warm smile moved across his face. He was always smiling and it irritated the heck out of me. One thing I knew for sure. I disliked morning people. They were perky.

"Good morning. Would you like a bath? The doctor said you could now that the bandages have been removed."

I almost groaned aloud.

"Yes, thank you. I could use a long soak with lots of bubbles. I love bubbles. Oh, and I love scented candles."

I felt a giddy excitement and jumped up and down.

"Caleb!" I grabbed his arm and he gave a start.

"What's wrong? Are you hurt?"

I dropped my hand and stood there, grinning like a fool. "No, nothing's wrong. I just remembered I like scented candles and long, hot baths."

He returned my grin. "Well, hot water and bubbles I can do, but I don't have any scented candles. Maybe on my next run into town I'll get you some."

I'd like to go to town. Someone might recognize me. "Can I go into town with you?"

He went into the bathroom and turned on the taps for my bath. His voice drifted out, "Sure. I'm not going for a couple of days. Maybe you'll be strong enough to come along for a change of scenery." He turned off the taps and came back into the bedroom. "Give me a shout when you're ready to come downstairs for breakfast."

Stretched out in the tub, the water lapped against my neck and shoulders, the bubbles creating a shimmering quilt upon the water. I let the soothing warmth remove any tension I felt. When I slid my hands over my body, I imagined that big hands were caressing me. The memory of tangy cologne tickled my senses.

An ache lodged itself in my heart. There was no ring on my finger, or even a tan line indicating I'd worn one, so I wasn't married. But I knew I'd had a lover. The question was, who? Caleb? I tried to picture him being intimate with me. It was possible. He had a great body. Hard and muscular, hidden beneath button down shirts.

What would he look like in a black tee shirt and faded Levis? In my distant memory I heard a whispered, *I've got you darlin'*. I leaned my head against the back of the tub and tried to follow that voice, but couldn't. There was nothing but darkness and a sense of great loss.

Caleb's voice came through the closed door. "Dixie, are you alright? I thought I heard you cry out."

With a start, I realized I'd been crying. My voice husky, I called out. "I'm okay. I'll be a few more minutes." I quickly finished bathing and as I toweled off, I realized I didn't have any decent clothes to change into. "Caleb?"

He must have been waiting right outside the door because he answered immediately, "Yes, are you alright?"

"That's getting old. You don't have to ask me every three seconds if I'm all right."

His voice let me know he was smiling when he answered, "Okay, what do you want?"

"Do I have any clothes? I mean, all I have is two nightgowns and a housecoat. Where are my clothes?" I tugged the freshly laundered nightgown over my head and brushed out my tangled curls.

"Give me a few minutes. I'll find something for you to wear."

Caleb returned with a pair of jeans and a cotton shirt, his face tingeing dull red when a lacy bra dangled out from under the shirt. He shifted his position at the door and said, "These are your jeans and underwear. The shirt's my sister's. It should fit; she was about your height. I'll be downstairs if you need anything. We'll have breakfast when you're ready."

Fortunately, everything fit fairly well, even if the jeans were a little loose. I guess being in a coma was also a great weight loss program. Soft moccasins were the only footwear available, so I slipped them on and headed downstairs for the first time since I'd awakened two weeks ago.

I was anxious to see what the rest of the house looked like. I couldn't put my finger on it, but nothing in the bedroom felt like it was mine. Maybe another room in the house would trigger a latent memory. The doctor, on his last visit, told me I'd suffered a major blow to the head which was why I couldn't remember who I was, or where I was from. He said my memory might return and it might not. The brain was a tricky thing. It marched to its own little drummer.

The old phrase *Today is the first day of the rest of your life*, spun through my head. How true. The journey to discover who I was had started. My stomach protested with a loud rumble.

Okay, the journey would start after breakfast.

****

I followed the smell of bacon to the kitchen where I found Caleb making breakfast.

"Mmmm, I think I love the smell of bacon and eggs." I stared at the scarred, wooden table, located smack dab in the middle of a typical country kitchen filled with lots of cupboards and counter space. It was the perfect spot for large family gatherings and baking scores of pies. I wondered if I baked pies.

Caleb said without turning around. "Have a seat. I'm almost done."

Though this was an older home, the finest of appliances graced this room. Judging by the smells making my stomach rumble Caleb knew how to use them too. So far, most of our meals had been prepared by Mrs. Cribbs, a local woman who came out four days a week to do housework and prepare meals. Today was her one of her days off.

He set a plate of bacon, eggs and toast in front of me, followed by a steaming cup of coffee.

"Do you take milk or sugar?"

My mind stayed blank. "I don't know. I'll try it black and add if I need to." I sipped my coffee and felt a familiar satisfaction. Lifting my cup in a mock salute I said, "Black."

"Aren't you going to eat?" Caleb had sat down and noticed me staring when he took a sip of his coffee.

"I need to thank you."

"For what?"

"For looking after me. I mean, who am I to you?"

"I'm not sure how much I should tell you." He set his coffee down. "You're in the Witness Protection Program. Do you know what that is?"

I nodded.

"You were hurt when your house was blown apart. It's a miracle you survived. Because you have no living relatives, we've allowed everyone, including whoever set the explosives, to think you are dead."

The words *no living relatives* sank in.

"Is my name even Dixie?" Tears welled up in my eyes, and I wiped them away with the back of my hand. I felt anger at this show of emotion. I knew I wasn't an emotional crier. This had to come from something deeper. Something I hadn't figured out, or remembered, yet.

"No, but because of your memory loss the doctor says it's better if you don't know it right now. If anyone calls you anything other than Dixie you'll know not to trust them. There's a reason why your mind has blocked all this and when you're ready, hopefully you'll have full recovery."

I reached across and took his calloused hand in mine. "Thank you, Caleb. You've been good to me."

He attacked his breakfast. Between mouthfuls he said, "Eat up. I don't want you to die from hunger after everything else that happened to you."

With gusto I dug in. Caleb wouldn't let me help with the dishes, so I wandered around and finally found what could be called a library. Rich, mahogany shelves filled with books from floor to ceiling covered one whole wall. A desk with a leather chair took advantage of natural light streaming in through the large window.

I plopped down on the big leather couch with a book, but after a few minutes I scooted over to the other end. Nothing felt right. Finally, I shifted over to the big comfy chair, snuggled in deep and swung my leg over the side. That was better.

By late afternoon I was extremely fatigued and headed for bed. Every step to the second floor pulled energy from my legs and drained me.

Caleb called from the living room, "Do you need a

hand?"

"No, I have to do this. I'll be all right. Good night."

I grabbed the railing and hauled myself up the last few steps. I heard a creak on the floor and knew he watched. He always watched. Probably waiting for me to tumble down these blasted stairs.

I stopped and caught my breath at the top. Sheesh. A baby kitten could take me right now. My legs shook, every step became an effort, but I made it to my room and collapsed on the bed, and fell asleep with my clothes on. Slow beginnings, but it heralded the start of my physical recovery. It took another week before I could stay up all day without nodding into my soup at supper.

One quiet evening Caleb and I were in the den. Seated at his desk he was going over bills and paperwork, chewing the end of his pen and scratching his head—a lot. Instinctively I know he didn't like to do bookwork. He was a hands-on kind of guy.

In my comfy chair I read a book his sister left behind, *The Immortal Highlander*. With a little tear in my eye from the happy ending, and a satisfied sigh I finished the book and looked over at Caleb.

A sense of déjà-vu washed over me, watching him in the lamp light. Without warning, a man's face, achingly familiar with its ruggedness and strength, darted in and out. I tried to grasp the memory, hold onto it and complete the picture with a name or even a place, but it faded back into obscurity. A pang of sadness settled over me, a feeling of something profound being lost.

What if I never got my memory back? Would I ever get used to my brain skipping liked a scratched record? That was too scary a thought so I decided to ignore the sliver of memory and instead, asked Caleb a question which nagged at me all day.

"Caleb?"

"Hmm?" His attention remained on the papers in front of him.

"What did I do?"

He put down his pen and looked over. "What do you mean?"

"I *mean*...what did I do for a living? I can't stay with you forever and I must have had a job. Doesn't anyone miss me?"

I asked this because earlier that afternoon I'd been sweeping off the front porch for the millionth time and as clear as a bell I'd seen myself standing on the corner of a busy street with two other girls. They'd asked a few drivers if they wanted dates and I saw money in my hand and then the memory door slammed shut.

It made me wonder, as always, what I did for a living. Had I been a hooker and I was in the Witness Protection Program because I'd seen some heinous crime while I plied my trade? Why else would I be in the company of two street walkers?

All day this question had festered and I needed answers.

After a brief pause he said. "You were a Private Investigator and handled mostly divorce cases and missing persons."

My shoulders sagged and I let out my breath in a soft whoosh. Aunt Tillie would've killed me if I'd have been a hooker. Instant joy flashed through me. I have an aunt. Caleb said I didn't have any family, but I know I have an aunt. I rolled her name around on my tongue, savoring it. Tillie. A tiny frisson of excitement coursed through my veins and I almost missed what Caleb said next.

"Your last case ran parallel with one of ours and you

got caught in the cross-fire. We believe the bomb was
directed at our agent staying at your house."

I went to twirl my hair, something I did when I was
thinking hard, but it was too short.

"Why would an agent be at my house? Was he hurt?"

"You two had a history. He was in town, following
leads and wasn't at the house at the time of the explosion. I
don't have any other details."

"So, I have nobody?"

Caleb nodded slowly. "The only other person involved
with you on a daily basis was your secretary and I don't have
any information on her."

"How long do you think I'll have to stay here?"

"I don't know, Dixie. Maybe a few weeks, months,
maybe only days. You shouldn't worry about that right now.
Concentrate on getting healthy."

I digested this information. Nothing, other than
knowledge of an aunt, had twigged a huge jolt of memory.
No choirs as I jumped to my feet singing, *Hallelujah, I got
my memory back!* Just an annoying blank curtain drawn tight
across my brain, with one small tear that Aunt Tillie crawled
through.

I wondered what she looked like.

"I'm off to bed." I stood and stretched. "Good night,
Caleb."

"Good night, Dixie."

From the window seat in my room, I gazed out over the
mountains, drew my knees close, and rocked slightly.
Maybe, just maybe, my life was trying to find me. For the
first time in weeks I felt a surge of hope and I clung to it like
it was my favorite teddy bear.

Chapter Sixteen

Tank slipped in behind a group of laughing people and as soon as he'd passed the bouncer, peeled off from the crowd and made his way down a long hall which led to private rooms. Keeping to the shadows he proceeded to the third door on the left and, without knocking, entered.

He almost backed out when he saw a half-naked woman gyrating on a small table in front of a man reclined on the couch. Until he realized the man was Rodie. Dressed in a vibrant purple silk jacket over an even brighter yellow shirt, Rodie, with a cheesy grin plastered on his face, watched the woman dance. Upon Tank entering, Rodie gestured at the woman to take some money he had in his hand and with a pat on the behind, sent her out of the room.

"You said you had to keep a low profile." Tank growled once the door was safely closed.

Rodie put his wallet back into his pocket. "Hey man, for me, this is low key. If I didn't go to a girlie club at least once a week my cover wouldn't stand up for nuthin'. They all think I'm a sleaze ball, so I sacrifice myself for the job."

He waved Tank over to a comfortable chair that faced the divan. Rodie's quick hand signal told him there were cameras in the room, no hidden microphones. Instantly on high alert Tank knew he had to follow Rodie's lead.

Rodie shrugged out of his brightly colored silk jacket.

"Did you bring it?"

He'd sent encoded instructions for Tank to bring a small baggie filled with a mixture of white sugar and flour. Nodding the affirmative, Tank pulled a clear bag out of his coat pocket and tossed it to him. Rodie opened the bag, licked his pinkie finger and stuck it in the powdery substance. After he pulled his finger back out, he tested the powder with the tip of his tongue. With a satisfied smile he rubbed his back gums with the innocuous mixture.

Tank relaxed a bit as this was a gambit they'd used once before. When they both hunkered down at the coffee table to 'snort' a little coke, Rodie would pass whatever information he had while their heads were close. Anyone watching would think they were doing a line together. What they wouldn't see was Rodie pushing the powder off the table with his hand as he 'inhaled' his portion.

With their heads almost touching, Rodie didn't waste any time.

"Word out is that Big Boss is a tad peeved about Regis and how everything went down. He also thinks your girl is alive."

The memory of Shelby's funeral squeezed Tank's heart. Even after six weeks, the hurt cut straight to his gut whenever he thought of her being lost to him forever.

"Yeah, well he wasn't the one who saw her in the coroner's car."

Rodie handed Tank a tightly rolled one hundred dollar bill and Tank took care of his line of flour.

"No man. He's convinced this was a set up and he's had a few of us looking into things. Like, who called the Coroner? We know the cops didn't, and EMS didn't, so how'd he get there so fast?"

Tank sat back on the chair and stared at Rodie. What

the…?. Had he been played? At the time he hadn't given any thought as to why her casket had never been open for visitation. Even if it had, he couldn't have brought himself to look at her laying there on the satin pillow. But if what Rodie said was true then it would make sense. The casket had stayed closed because there was no body to be buried.

Not realizing what Tank was thinking, Rodie continued talking as he sealed the remaining powder in the baggie. "And here's another interesting fact. Immediately after the explosion, neighbors reported Shelby had been cared for by a concerned passer-by. A passer-by who conveniently knew CPR, told everyone Shelby didn't survive the blast and covered her face with his jacket."

Thinking fast Tank leaned toward Rodie. "How many people are on to this?"

"Me and Gizmo. I wouldn't worry too much about him. He's lazy and hates getting his hands dirty, if you know what I mean. Besides, with Big Boss still lying low, Gizmo don't do much more than call dial-a-pussy."

Tank held out his hand as if expecting money and when Rodie pulled a wad of bills out of his pocket he asked, "Any leads on Big Boss?"

Rodie laid the money in Tank's palm. "Last I heard someone said he's holed up in Taiwan, but I've got a hunch he's closer to home. I think he's in the Caymans, biding his time until he can come back stateside. He lost a good chunk of revenue when we snagged Regis."

Tank stood. "That's a fact. Regis made a lot of money for the scumbag. Thanks Rodie. I'm gonna check out my sources. Stay safe."

Rodie leaned back on the couch and spread his arms across the back, kicking his feet out on the now clean coffee table. When he grinned wide Tank saw he'd added a gold cap to his left incisor. His voice sounded amused. "Don't I always stay safe, T-man?"

Tank opened the door and Rodie called out, "Send in my women. I feel the need for some lovin'. Rodie's lonely in here."

Tank stepped aside and allowed two scantily clad women to pass by him into the room. As the door closed he heard them giggle and an answering chuckle from Rodie.

****

When a little over six weeks had passed and the doctor gave me the thumbs up to start exercising again I asked Caleb if he'd teach me some self-defense. I'd seen him working a punching bag in his gym over the garage and thought he could give me a few pointers.

To my surprise he agreed.

Nervousness in the shape of a thousand butterflies fluttered around in my stomach. It was only a little bit of self-defense but what if he accidentally caught me in the face and knocked out a tooth? Or worse, broke my nose.

When I entered the gym I almost choked to stop myself from laughing. Louis, one of Caleb's ranch hands, had on what looked like a baseball catcher's vest. Caleb told me I was going to punch, kick, and hit Louis and the suit would protect him. Louis looked utterly miserable.

"You okay with this Louis?"

Louis shifted from one foot to the other, a trickle of sweat edging its way down the side of his face under what had to be a padded catcher's mask.

"Yup. Boss said I'd get a weekend off if I did this for ya."

"Good deal, Louis, but I'd have held out for a week."

I could tell by the widening of his eyes he wished he'd

thought of that too. Next time, if there was a next time, I knew he'd bargain harder.

Caleb stood in front of me and showed me how to hold my fist, the best way to maximize the punch without expending too much energy and stay on my feet.

"Okay. Now I want you to punch Louis in the stomach."

Louis braced himself for the hit.

I did my best Mohamed Ali footwork and pretended to be ducking some jabs, then without thought I let a punch fly straight for Louis' gut. The force of the hit surprised everyone and Louis fell hard, with a loud groan. I rushed to Louis and tried to help him up.

Caleb reached out and pulled my shoulder, to move me out of the way. The next thing I knew Caleb was flat out on the floor staring up at me after I'd flipped him over my back.

"Holy Mackeral, Caleb. Are you okay?"

Louis, forgotten, rolled away from us, and I fell to my knees beside Caleb.

"Caleb. Are you okay, did I hurt you?"

He pushed up onto his elbows and stared at me.

"I don't think I have to teach you any defensive moves. You appear to have yourself well in hand," came the dry reply.

I looked over at Louis who was still struggling to get off the floor in that ridiculous padded outfit and then down at Caleb lying beside me. Before I could think about it I started to giggle. The more I tried to stop and look remorseful, the harder I laughed. One little woman had just laid two men out flat without even trying.

I knew he didn't want to, but a smile pulled at the corner of Caleb's mouth. I stood and offered my hand. Ignoring it, he stood and dusted off his jeans.

"Come on, Dixie. Let's get Louis out of that oversized rubber band and see if you can shoot."

The gym disappeared and the distinctive odor of carbine burned the back of my nose. I held a tiny pink gun, I called it my baby. It had very little kick back and target, floating at the end of a padded gun range, showed a perfect circle of bullet holes where the heart would be.

"Dixie."

These flashes were becoming weird.

"Dixie!" Caleb shook my shoulders.

"What?"

"You lost all your color and your eyes glazed over. What happened?"

I tried to recall the details, but once again everything just danced around the edges of my memory, teasing me. I shrugged away from Caleb's grip. "Nothing. A memory, but I don't think you have to show me how to shoot. Something tells me I'd do okay."

"You sure?"

"Yeah," I sighed. "As sure as I am about everything else. Can you help Louis? I'm going to head back to the house. My head hurts a bit." I wanted to lie down before nausea set in. Lately the headaches made me sick to my stomach.

"Sure, Dixie. I'll see you at supper."

****

I'm standing on the beach and watch the light of the full moon glimmer across the water. A soft summer breeze lifts the hair off my neck and I appreciate its coolness. A pretty blonde woman grabs my arm. She's pointing out three men on the other side of the bon-fire. I immediately recognize Caleb, but not the other two. I'm angry that I can't remember who they are.

All three men are handsome, but the one furthest from me stands apart, in both looks and size. My awareness of him is instantaneous. He meets my curious gaze with bold eyes and I can feel myself blush. Instinctively, I wrap my arms around my midsection and break eye contact. Shivers of awareness cause the hairs on my arms to stand on end.

A voice, whiny and needy grates in my ear and I feel a sense of urgency. I turn to leave and I bump into someone, losing my balance. Large hands steady me and I look up. It's the stranger from across the fire. Although his face is concealed by shadows, I catch a playful, roguish smile. Dark hair, a little long, brushes his shoulders. The fear and loneliness flee when he kisses me with a hunger that has my heart pounding. Heat lances through me, from head to toe, and brands me for life. I am his.

I'm on a beach again and it's now a beautiful sunny day. The man with the dangerous smile walks with me, our fingers laced together. My heart flies as free as the birds swooping down to tease the ocean spray before soaring away.

In a tangle of legs and arms, we fall to the ground, his mouth warm on my stomach and I watch his dark head move slowly down my body. When he reaches the very core of me, I shatter into a million pieces and cry out his name.

Tank!

I jerked awake and flung aside the duvet. The covers were all twisted and my clothes clung to me. The now familiar dream, although a bit disjointed had been so real that I ached low in my belly.

I swung my feet over the side of the bed and sat for a bit to get my bearings. A few things were evident from this dream. One: Pieces of my memory were finally pushing through the fog. Two: I had a blond-haired friend. And three: I had a Tank.

Chapter Seventeen

When I'd been on the ranch almost two months, Mrs. Cribbs said I had potential. Potential for killing everything in the garden, that is.

She faithfully showed me which plants were edible and which ones you pulled. My back ached from being stooped over, so I took a mini-break and sat back on my haunches to look at the pile of pulled weeds.

"Are you sure these are weeds?"

They looked exactly like the ones still protruding out of the ground.

She looked over from a few rows away where she picked raspberries. "Yes dear, except the one at your knee. If you look closely you'll see little potatoes."

Sure enough, baby potatoes dangled from the big green leaves I'd ruthlessly tugged out of the ground. Oh dear. Brushing dirt off my knees I stood and pressed a hand to my back.

Gardening was hard work and the patch Caleb had at the back of his house was huge. We'd spent the last week peeling and dicing strawberries and rhubarb for pies. Some were in the freezer, but most had gone to the bake sale at Mrs. Cribbs' church. Mrs. Cribbs promised to show me how to can raspberries and make jelly.

I heard the familiar clip-clop of a horse on the gravel

drive and turned. Caleb swung up the drive and cantered toward us. He sat the horse well. Broad shoulders, cowboy hat, muscular thighs gripping either side of the roan stallion. Shading my eyes I watched him. Leather creaked when he leaned toward me, resting his tanned forearm on the saddle horn.

"I've got good news, Dixie."

My breath stopped in my throat.

"There's been a break in the case and you can go home."

Home? This was my home. A bubble of panic rose and I squashed it down as best I could. Faking a smile I said, "That *is* good news. We should celebrate."

He swung off the horse and holding the reins loosely, stood over me. He chucked his leather-gloved hand under my chin. "That's exactly what I thought. What do you think about going to the town dance with me?"

I looked over at Mrs. Cribbs, but she tactfully kept busy with the raspberries. A dance? Moving together in close contact? To music? I stammered out, "Uh, yeah. I mean, yes. I'd love to go to a dance."

A slow smile lifted the corner of his mouth, "Great. It's a date."

He pivoted and placing one foot in the stirrup, swung himself easily onto the back of the big horse. He dipped his hat at me, "Dixie," and then Mrs. Cribbs. "Ma'am." He clicked his tongue in the back of his throat and turned the roan toward the stables.

"Caleb, wait!" I called out and he pulled up on the horse. Twisting in the saddle, he looked back at me and grinned as I tripped over the little spade I'd been using to dig at helpless green, living plants. Pushing my hair out of my face I asked. "What was the break in the case?"

"Didn't I tell you?"

"No. My memory lapses are from *before* I got here, not *while* I've been here."

He grinned further. "We know who bombed your house and an arrest has been made. We're confident you can return home soon."

Chewing my lip I digested this latest piece of news. This was good news. Wasn't it?

"Anything else?" He patted the horse's neck as it whinnied and stomped, anxious to move again.

"Nope. Thanks for the invite to the dance."

"You're more than welcome, Ma'am." He pressed his heels on the sides of the roan and cantered off, whistling a tuneless song.

Mrs. Cribbs made a choking sound and I looked over to see her ample bosom jiggling from barely suppressed laughter.

"What?" I turned back to watch Caleb, disappearing down the road that led to the stables.

She tried to smother her laughter, but it echoed in every word, "Oh dear. He sure put on a show. Made me think of Gary Cooper in *High Noon*, the way he rode up, calling me ma'am."

"Yeah, I guess he did at that. He sure looked good on the horse."

Mrs. Cribbs smiled. "Yes, he sure did. Reminded of my late husband, Gerry. God rest his soul." She picked up her full basket of raspberries and started walking to the house. "I guess we should go shopping. It's only a few days until the dance."

Confusion must have shown on my face because she laughed again and said, "You can't wear what you got on to the dance. We have to find you the right dress, a nice pair of boots and get your hair cut. Come on." She put her arm around my waist, "I know just the place to take you."

I don't know what scared me more. Going on a quasi-date with Caleb or shopping for a pair of boots with Mrs. Cribbs.

****

"You look divine!" The salesclerk gushed.

I cast a wry eye over the outfit in question. I may look like a dumb blonde, but no way would I dress like one. *Julianna*, my personal stylist, insisted I pour myself into a slinky red leather dress which left very little to the imagination and could double as a rain slicker if required. She then produced a pair of mile-high stilettos and cooed that my boyfriend would *simply adore* me in them.

Caleb had given me his platinum card to shop with and after a quick call to make sure it wasn't stolen, I'd been subjected to speculative glances all afternoon.

I looked at the sultry siren reflected in the mirror and was suddenly tired of being nice to a woman who obviously thought I was being kept in the wrong sense of the word. This was just one more moment where I wished I had my own job and money and identity. I pulled the curtain and poked my head out.

"Julianna."

She scurried over to my dressing room.

"Find me something quiet and understated. Something *you* would never wear. I also need a pair of shoes that are chic and not over three inches." Pivoting, I ignored her outraged gasp and drew the dressing room curtain closed. I tugged and pulled the dress over my head and hung it back up. The three dimensional mirror allowed me to see my whole body and I noticed a mark at the top of my hip.

Twisting as far as I could, my back to the mirror, I stared at the tattoo which looked like a T, with an artsy heart wrapped around it. I never thought I'd be the kind of girl who had a tattoo, but apparently I was. Maybe I *should* wear the come hither dress. Either that or a leather jacket with chains because I was a biker chick, although I didn't feel like one. A quick check revealed no more inked art and I was torn between relief and disappointment.

Maybe my name started with the letter T. I rolled a few names on my tongue to see if they sounded familiar. Theresa, Tara, Tiffany. None felt right. Tracey? Taylor? Trish? I sighed in frustration. None of them triggered name memories. Maybe I'd gotten a tattoo for the elusive Aunt Tillie.

Julianna returned and with an elegant sniff handed me a few more dresses and a pair of beige pumps.

"Thank you." I poked my head around the curtain, again. "Would you please see if the woman I was with has returned?"

Mrs. Cribbs had gone to make a hair appointment for me at one of the most expensive salons in town. Ignoring my protests, she insisted on booking me with Raymonde, who according to an ebullient Julianna had a waiting list ten years long. Apparently he worked with Caleb before he hung up his sniper rifle and picked up tinting gel.

I pulled a navy slip dress over my shoulders and settled it around my waist. It had a nice flare at the hips and when I twisted from side to side the skirt swirled around my legs. The ugly pumps would have to be changed to bright red and I could already envision a red belt and earrings completing the outfit. I'd found my dress for the town dance.

After changing back into my jeans and tee shirt Julianna informed me Mrs. Cribbs had returned and my hair appointment was in fifteen minutes. I rushed to lace my running shoes, grabbed my bag of clothes and found Mrs. Cribbs waiting patiently for me.

"Come on, dear. We only have a few minutes." She took the bag from me and with amazing speed for a woman her size, barreled through shoppers like an offensive tackle heading for the quarterback. I slid into her slipstream and allowed her drag me along.

****

After weeks of careful digging and a quiet call to someone higher up in the Agency, Tank discovered Shelby was in the Witness Protection Program and Neil was heading it. In the half hour it took him to drive to Neil's office he worked himself into a quiet fury.

Barging into Neil's office, followed closely by his secretary Bette, Tank enjoyed the look of irritation that swept across Neil's narrow face.

"I'm sorry, Mr.—" Bette apologized.

Neil stopped her with a dismissive wave of his hand. "That's fine Bette. I'll handle it."

Bette backed out of the office and closed the door quietly behind her. Tank stalked toward Neil's desk, wanting nothing more than to grab him by his scrawny neck and squeeze. Sheer willpower had Tank loosen his fists, determined not to lose his temper. His voice was deadly quiet when he asked Neil.

"Where is she?"

"I'm in a meeting, Steele. Come back when you've calmed down.

Tank glanced over his shoulder and was surprised to see Liz seated in the plush leather seat facing Neil's desk. A rueful look on her face, she shrugged her shoulders.

Mentally, he dismissed her. His mission was to find out where, exactly, Shelby had been placed.

He squared his shoulders. "Your meeting just got a little bigger. I'm not going anywhere until you tell me where she is. Don't make me lose my temper, Neil. You don't like me when I'm angry."

There was a long pause before Neil said, "Take a seat."

Tank slid into the leather chair beside Liz and tried to relax when all he wanted to do was race out and search for Shelby. She was out there somewhere. Living, laughing, and breathing.

Without him.

Tank watched Neil straighten some papers and place them neatly in a folder on his desk. His deliberate ploy to gain control of the situation made Tank's blood boil. Tank leaned forward in his chair. "Where is she and why didn't you tell me?"

Neil pushed back from his desk and assessed Tank through narrowed eyes. He tapped the folder on his desk. "She's in the WPP. You know the rules."

"Bull shit!" Tank rose to his feet. Liz placed a restraining hand on his arm and tried to pull him back into his seat. Tank glared at Neil. "You didn't tell me because you didn't want the case compromised. You're a pencil-pushing, corporate whore."

"Tank—" Liz interjected.

He looked sideways at her. Tank realized the folder on the desk was Shelby's case and that could only mean Neil and Liz had been discussing her. Had they ever planned on telling him she was alive? All those months he'd crawled into a bottle Liz had known and said nothing.

His lip curled in a sneer. "You're no better, lady. You were in on it. Did Neil pimp you out to get me back on the case?"

"You're off base Steele and you know it. Liz did not create this situation." Neil's quiet voice cut like a knife through Tank's anger. He shrugged off Liz's hand and sat back in the chair.

Neil waited a few moments. "We sent an agent to the house. The plan was to put her into protective custody until the heat died down, but when he got there it was too late. She'd already been knocked unconscious from flying debris."

Tank remembered all the bits of board and plaster that had covered the driveway.

"He posed as a concerned passer-by and kept neighbors away and called for backup. The Coroner is one of ours. He took the call and attended the scene. You were the wild card. Everything almost fell apart when you showed up, demanding to see the body."

It sickened Tank when he thought about how close he'd been to her and hadn't realized she was alive. He'd touched her. He should have known.

He had only one question when Neil was finished.

"Where—exactly—is she?"

Chapter Eighteen

Loud music blared through the open doors of the town dance hall. Half-ton trucks, SUV's and flashy cars filled the parking lot. Laughing couples and crowds of friends created a living river of people that flowed through the doors and spilled out onto the street. It looked like everyone from the town and surrounding county had come to *the* dance, ready to party.

My step was light and I caught myself bouncing on the balls of my feet waiting for Caleb to lock the truck. We'd managed to snag the last parking spot at the back of the lot. The music called to me and I couldn't wait to dosey-do a few rounds. Caleb had better be a good dancer or he was in serious trouble.

This dance dominated my thoughts ever since Caleb invited me. I felt like I was in high school again when Mrs. Cribbs and I went to the 'big city' to find a dress and get my hair cut and styled. She'd wanted me to buy a pair of cowgirl boots but although I had country in my heart it would not be on my feet. Snappy sandals completed my outfit.

My hair had grown enough that I could catch it up in a clip with a few stray curls around my forehead to hide the tiny scar. The only visible souvenir from the explosion.

Caleb, as always, looked delicious. He had on a crisp cotton shirt and dark jeans. Normally his boots were scuffed and well-worn, but tonight he'd exchanged them for a pair of glossy black ones that shone. How he wasn't married yet baffled me. Daggered looks were thrown my way, but I ignored them all and twined my arm through his. We walked to a table, near the back door, and pulling out a chair he said, "Would you like a drink, Dixie?"

"Sure what do they have?" I plunked myself on the sturdy, wooden chair.

He looked over to the bar and said, "I see beer.... beer.... more beer and a poor imitation of wine."

"Well...let me see." I cocked my head to one side and pretended to study the bar. "Let's try the beer."

He grinned. "Good choice. I'll be right back."

He proceeded to the bar, his stride confident. The men milling around shook his hand and it was obvious that Caleb was respected and liked by others. After a short time I looked around the hall. My attention drifted to a group of girls watching me and then leaning into one another, whispering. One finally stood and came over. She had a determined look on her face and all I could think was—this could be fun.

"Hi. I'm Sissy."

"Hello, Sissy." I replied, not blinking an eye. Without asking she sat across from me and waited for me to introduce myself. But I wasn't ready to divulge any information to a stranger. Like Caleb said, if they didn't call me Dixie, they didn't know me. Anyone who didn't know me could be a potential threat.

"I've seen you around town." She continued after the awkward pause. "You're staying at the Circle K Ranch."

I nodded and found it interesting that this wasn't posed as a question. It took all my self-control not to sneak a peek at the bar, wondering how long Caleb would be and where she would take the conversation.

"Are you family?" She asked.

Now I smiled. Old fashioned jealousy was something I could identify with. I didn't bother to reason how I knew about jealousy; I just knew that I did.

"Nope. Caleb's a friend." With perfect timing, the object of our conversation returned, and set the beers on the table. Droplets of condensation ran down the outside of the bottles.

"Hey Sissy. How's your brother? Haven't seen him in ages."

Sissy flushed and stammered out, "Brandon's re-enlisted and gone back overseas. He should be home this time next year."

"That's good to hear. Say hi to him for me. Look, I don't mean to be rude, but I promised Dixie a dance." He held out his hand and I slipped mine into it, allowing him to pull me onto the dance floor leaving Sissy pouting at the table.

We'd spun around a few times in perfect unison when I said, "That was rude, Caleb."

He sighed and twirled me under his arm, settling it back on my shoulder, moving forward in time with the two-step. "I know. Sissy's had a school girl crush on me for as long as I can remember. I try not to encourage her..." He let the sentence trail off. I knew exactly what he was talking about. Regis never took a hint either.

Who was Regis? Although this was another mystery person, the name gave me shivers, and not in a good way.

****

The DJ called out 'last dance' and we joined a dozen other couples. Drawing me closer, Caleb's hand felt warm on my back, his other holding mine. *Carrying Your Love With Me* played softly and we swayed to the music around the crowded dance floor.

Somehow we made our way into a quiet, secluded corner. When I realized where we were, I looked up at Caleb. His face was angles and chiseled planes. I'd always thought he had the look of a man who could make hard decisions. A man who would protect me, always.

But right now he didn't look like he wanted to protect me, because he kept staring at my mouth. I heard him whisper, "I've wanted to do this for years."

One big hand cupped the back of my head and the other held my hand against his hard chest, trapped between our bodies. He dipped his head and was going to kiss me. I froze in panic. No, no, no. This was all wrong. I shouldn't be kissing another man. I pushed at his chest and he stopped, inches from my lips. For a moment regret flickered in his eyes, but it was gone so fast I couldn't be sure.

"I'm sorry, Caleb. Nothing against you, but this doesn't feel right. I don't know why, but I feel like I'm being unfaithful."

He slid me a look that was hard to decipher and then nodded. His quiet voice carried above the music and peoples voices in the dance hall. "I know. Come on. It's time we headed home anyway."

We moved off the dance floor and stepped outside. Caleb ploughed into my back when I stopped suddenly. He grabbed my shoulders to stop me from falling face first in the gravel walk. "What the…?"

The edges of my vision blurred and everything closed in around me. I felt myself begin to slump in his arms and fumbled to grab onto anything that would keep me upright. Caleb wrapped his arms around my middle and huffed me closer to his chest.

"Dixie?"

I struggled to hold onto his voice, but he slipped further and further away. I concentrated on my breathing. I would *not* faint in front of the whole town. Not. Going. To. Happen.

Breathe. In through my nose, out through my mouth.

Breathe. In, two three. Out, two, three.

Slowly, the dizziness subsided, but I still had a queasy feeling of nausea. Caleb by now had carried me to his truck. He reached out and lowered the tailgate before sitting on it, settling me on his lap.

"Dixie. What just happened?"

"I don't know," I said and shuddered.

He started to rub my arms, trying to warm me up. Why did I almost pass out? Trying to remember brought fresh pain behind my eyes, but I pushed through the fog, determined to get past this and move on. This almost fainting crap was starting to tick me off.

A brief vignette played across my memory. As Caleb and I stepped outside, one of the local girls crawled into a huge truck cab and I saw the back of a man's hand when he opened the door. The tattoo inked across it was a snake. When his hand moved the snake twisted and turned around the bones. I'd seen a tattoo like that before, I just didn't know where or when.

What I *did* know was an instinctive reaction to run and not look back.

"I guess the dance was more than I could handle. I'm not as strong as I thought."

"I'm sorry. I should have known better." He set me on my feet and steered me over to the passenger side of the truck. "Hop in, we're going home. You've had enough for one night."

I wanted to say, 'No, let's go for drinks or a coffee.' But my head hurt and tiredness swept through me, draining any energy I may have had in reserve. So I nodded yes and climbed into the truck, falling asleep before we were out of the parking lot.

****

"Dixie." Caleb shook my shoulder, "We're home."

I opened my eyes, yawned and stretched and saw we were parked by his house. Caleb opened his door, but my hand on his forearm stopped him from leaving the vehicle.

"Caleb, wait. You said you'd wanted to kiss me for years. I've only been here for a few months. Mind explaining that to me."

I thought he'd never answer he took so long. "I wished I'd met you first."

"First? What do you mean?"

He sighed heavily. "It's a long story. You and another girl were at a beach party a couple of years ago. Before I had a chance to even meet you, Ta—, Jake had you in his sights."

"Jake?"

"He was my partner. We were in town on a case and after he met you, he told the bosses he'd relocate to the Chicago office. He wasn't going anywhere. You got married real fast, lived together for about a year and then split. You were working the case with him, and I don't know much more than that. I haven't heard from him in months."

"So this Jake, he's the agent who was staying at my house when the explosion happened?"

"Yeah, we got him away from the house in time, but not you. I've been told he was pretty torn up."

This made me feel better. At least someone cared I'd died. "Does he know I'm alive?"

"No one knows you're alive except me, the WPP team and my immediate supervisor. We have to do that, for your own safety."

"Will Jake be told, now that there's been a break in the case?"

Caleb opened his door and turned to look at me through the cab, his expression hidden in the dark. "Most likely. There'd be no reason to keep it a secret."

Walking into the house and to my room I thought about what Caleb said. I'd been married, to Jake, which meant I must have loved him at one time. One would assume we'd been intimate. So, why couldn't I bring his face to mind?

And saying the name Jake was like saying Tom, Dick, or Harry. I sighed and got ready for bed. Tomorrow was a big day. Mrs. Cribbs, satisfied with my burgeoning culinary skills, was finally going to part with her prize winning jelly recipe. I could taste the sweetness already.

Teeth brushed, night cream on, I crawled into bed. My mind was drifting and I was at that stage where you're almost asleep, when I slammed awake.

The beach party from my dream!

Caleb said he first saw me at a beach party and I'd been dreaming about that for weeks. Could the man I'd seen myself walking and making love with be Jake? If he was, why did I cry out the name Tank? I punched my pillow into a different shape and tried to go to sleep.

Tank, that wasn't a name, it was a thing. I mean, really, who called themselves Tank?

I sat up again. Caleb stumbled over Jake's name. He'd started to say one that started with the letter 'T'. My hand instinctively went to my hip, touching the tattoo. Could it stand for Tank? Groaning, I flopped back onto my pillow. I'd apparently been married to an undercover agent, who'd probably killed—I stopped right there. If my world got any more twisted, I'd have to write a book. No one lived this kind of life. It was too surreal.

I lay for a long time, waiting for sleep to steal me away.

Chapter Nineteen

Tank's heart raced while he drove through the picturesque town that lay outside of Caleb's ranch, The Circle K. He was familiar with the town and the ranch since he'd been Caleb's partner for over eight years. He recognized the grocery mart where they probably still delivered groceries to your home. Same old furniture store, church, local courthouse and Sheriff's office, with a big hound dog sprawled out front. The dog lifted its head and gave Tank a lethargic look when he cruised by. Probably the same old dog too.

A sign by the side of the road pointed to the Circle K Ranch and he followed the shaded drive that would lead him to Shelby. His stomach churned and he could barely breathe. Before he left Neil's office, Neil told him Shelby had amnesia and in the last report from Caleb, hadn't regained her memory.

What if she never remembered him? He'd been in Special Forces and gone into numerous high-risk areas, but the fear crawling along his spine right now was something he never experienced.

After cresting a small hill, he saw the house and pulled alongside. Fear anchored him to the seat. For every mile he'd driven, a different scenario played inside his mind. She could look at him and smile politely, because he was a stranger. Or she could hide, because Caleb warned her not to trust strangers. But the one scenario that gripped his heart and squeezed was the thought that she could look at him with indifference. Not because she didn't remember him but because she had, and didn't want him in her life.

He removed the photo of him and Shelby from his wallet. Already softening around the edges, he caressed Shelby's image with his finger. Hopefully, he'd have the real thing in his arms today. Finally he folded the photo and tucked it back into his wallet and stepped out of the rental car.

With a deep breath he mounted the front steps of the porch and pushed open the screen door. Music floated through the air and he followed the sound to the kitchen, stopping in the doorway. Her back to him, she hummed aloud while moving to the lively beat, hair bouncing around her shoulders. She grabbed a dish from the drying rack beside the sink and swiped a tea towel over the brightly patterned plate.

Even he didn't recognize his voice when he finally uttered her name.

"Shelby."

****

A deep, hoarse voice lifted above the music, calling my name. There was pain in that solitary word. I continued to dry the dish and looked toward the door. There he stood, gaunter than I remembered, his face tired and drawn, eyes hollow.

"Hi Tank." I pivoted to put the dish in the cupboard and it fell from nerveless fingers, clipping the counter before smashing against the hardwood floor. Like a movie playing in slow motion, I turned to face the man I thought I'd never forget, but had.

I couldn't move. I only stared. It was him, the man from my dreams. A sensation like a battering ram pummeled my temple as the floodgates opened and everything I'd blocked rushed in.

Every time I blinked a new memory hit, making each breath difficult. It was Christmas and we were opening presents with my mom and Aunt Tillie. Then blink, a different memory of Tank's arms wrapped around me, my heart breaking as the doctor unplugged my mother's life support. Another blink and Tank walked away while I cried and pleaded with him to stay.

Caleb came through the door and stood behind Tank, his face wary. I knew I was falling to the floor because I watched them both rush to catch me before I hit.

****

"Why didn't anyone call me? She's my wife."

"You were separated. Everyone thought you were only working the case."

"I thought she was dead! You guys let me think she was dead."

Lying on the couch I listened to Caleb and Tank arguing. Although they kept their voices low, it still carried into the living room.

More memories bounced around and this time I held onto them. I saw Tank kissing my fingers, telling me he was back for good and how he'd left to protect me. I recalled how relieved I'd felt, but after that I couldn't remember anything more. Had we made up? Had I dreamed it?

They continued to argue in the hall. Should I let them know I could hear them? Deciding against it I closed my eyes. I wasn't ready to face either of them yet. What I hadn't counted on was Mrs. Cribbs.

"She can hear you two morons." Mrs. Cribbs passed by the living room on the way to the kitchen. "Take it outside if you're going to squabble. She don't need this right now."

Between Mrs. Cribbs ratting me out and the sound of me shifting on the couch they knew I was awake. Both men entered the living room, Caleb looking apprehensive, Tank devastated. Tank came over and knelt beside me and I couldn't help it, I flinched when he caressed the side of my face. Hurt flashed in his odd colored eyes.

"They told me you had died."

"I'm sorry," I whispered. I didn't know what else to say.

Wouldn't his life be easier if I were dead? He'd left me without explanation and I meant nothing to him. Or did I? He seemed pretty concerned for a hardhearted ex-husband. This was all confusing. There was too much, too soon. I needed time to work through my jumbled memories.

"When can I go home and be me again?" I asked Caleb.

"Darlin'—" Tank started.

"I'm not your darling." He withdrew his hand from my hair he'd been stroking. "I'm not your anything."

I laid my head back against the couch and closed my eyes. A nagging pain pulsed behind them.

"You can go home anytime, Dix— Shelby. Your papers will take a bit of time and your house needs to be repaired." Caleb soothed.

"*Our* house is repaired." Tank bit out.

"Oh." Caleb was surprised; I could hear it in his voice. Against my better judgement, I smiled. Now I remembered how Tank got his name. When he wanted something, he could be very determined and single-minded and rolled over anything that got in his way.

I guess he would have fixed the damage. The house *was* his, after all. I'd moved in after we got married. For all I knew, he could have sold it by now. Why would he want to stay there anyway? Where would Polly and I watch movies?

"Polly!" I jolted upright. Caleb started forward and Tank reached out to steady me. I swatted his hand away and swung my legs to sit. "I have to call Polly. She thinks I'm dead!"

"We all thought you were dead." Tank's voice, full of hurt, washed over me. Maybe his apology before I'd been blasted by the bomb had been reality not a dream. I glanced down at my hands and was surprised to see them shaking.

I clasped them together and said, "Caleb, would you give Tank and me a few minutes?"

Caleb stepped out and I shuffled over on the couch to give Tank room. He slid in, but didn't try to crowd me or make me feel uncomfortable. I couldn't look at him. What do you say to someone who thought you had died? Someone you didn't know if you were mad at and wanted to punch in their handsome, unshaven face or someone you were ecstatic to see and wanted to leap into their arms and rain kisses all over that same handsome, unshaven face.

I couldn't look at him. I was afraid of what I'd see.

"Shelby."

I kept my head bowed.

"Shelby, look at me." The gentleness in his voice compelled me to turn my head and reluctantly I raised my eyes. He was smiling, genuinely smiling, even with his eyes. To say I was shocked would have been an understatement. With the tip of his finger, he tapped the bottom of my chin to close my mouth. He cupped my cheek with his hand, his wry smile tugging at my heart.

"You are so beautiful... I needed to see you, to touch

you." He removed his hand from my cheek and I felt a moment of loss and wanted him to touch me again. "I don't know what, or how much you remember and I don't care. I'd rather have you alive and hating me than not have you around at all. When they buried—" His voice roughened and broke. A tear squeezed out of his blue eye.

Tank never cried.

He laughed, he joked and he got mad. He never cried. Without thinking I brushed away his tear, and cupped his cheek in my palm. Close to tears myself, I swallowed hard.

After a brief pause he cleared his throat. "When they buried you, they may as well have placed me in the casket too. All of me was with you." He took hold of my hand and pressed it to the center of his chest. "You are my heart. Without you, I don't exist."

I couldn't constrain them anymore. Tears streamed down my cheeks and he wiped them away, never removing his gaze from mine. He'd just bared his soul and I was swimming in a sea of emotions.

Gathering me close he pressed my head against his chest. His thundering heart matched mine. As we sat, his heart rate slowed and became a steady, soothing beat. I didn't want to leave this cocoon of silence, this tiny life raft in the midst of all the confusion where I felt safe, truly safe for the first time in months.

This was where I belonged. I gave my heart wings and allowed myself to love him again.

Chapter Twenty

A lone suitcase rested at the foot of the stairs, filled with the few belongings I'd gathered in my short time at the ranch. Caleb bought it a few days ago when the decision had been made for me to go back home and pick up the pieces of my former life. Tank wandered off while I said my good-byes.

Even that surprised me. Since he arrived two days ago, he hadn't let me out of his sight. Last night I tripped over him when I got up to get a drink of water. He'd fallen asleep propped against the wall outside my bedroom, his long legs stretched across the hallway. Even though I loved Tank, I wasn't ready to sleep with him and besides, it didn't feel right to do that in Caleb's home. Also, I needed time to sort through feelings and memories that were jumbled together like a 1000-piece puzzle.

The inevitable phone call to Polly had been an adventure all by itself. She squealed, she giggled and she cried, all in the space of thirty seconds. I knew she'd be camped on my front porch waiting. Best friends since grade school, we hadn't been apart for longer than a few weeks as kids, except when her Daddy would take them to Europe in the summer. We talked for hours and she filled in the gaps Tank and Caleb wouldn't, or couldn't tell me, about Regis.

Regis kept insisting, to anyone who'd listen, that the

bomb was only supposed to scare Tank off, but I hadn't been born last night. The triggering device hadn't been on a timer. Someone pressed the detonation button. And that someone waited until Tank was gone and I was near the flash point.

Regis had decided that if he couldn't have me, then no one would. It was sheer luck I'd paused when I spotted the wire and hadn't been any closer to the immediate blast. Whatever made him think he had any claim on me was a mystery. I'd rebuffed him from the time we were eight. Even as a child he gave me chills.

The sound of banging crockery told me Mrs. Cribbs was in the kitchen. I paused in the door and watched her washing dishes in the oversized kitchen sink.

"Mrs. Cribbs?"

She turned, her eyes red-rimmed, and looked my way. Tears for me?

"Mrs. Cribbs. Don't cry."

She grabbed the corner of her apron and wiped her face. "I can cry if I want to. You kinda grew on me, girl." Efficiently, she turned back to the sink and set a frying pan on the drying rack.

At first, the smell from the breakfast spread on the table made my tummy flip-flop. I'd suffered from migraines and severe nausea the first few weeks on the ranch, and for the most part they'd gone away. The added strain of getting my memory back must have caused them to return, or at least the familiar queasiness at the smell of food.

"Did Tank have breakfast?" I loaded my plate with a bit of egg and dry toast.

"Yes. He said he was going down to the barn. Caleb's prize filly, Shay, is fixin' to drop her foal soon and he can't leave her." She waved her dish rag at me. "Eat now."

Obediently I scooped the fluffy egg into my mouth and

groaned. How does she do it? I could mimic every step and my food never melted in your mouth like hers. Maybe it was a good thing I was going home. A few more months of Mrs. Cribbs home cooking and I'd have to increase my ten mile run to twenty to melt off the pounds. As it was, my jeans were hard to close after a few months of her food.

I drained my coffee, wiped toast crumbs off my mouth and pushed back from the table. Mrs. Cribbs, scouring pans in the big ceramic farmers sink gave a start when I tapped her on the shoulder. Awkwardly she accepted the impulsive hug I threw around her.

"Thank you, Mrs. Cribbs." I stepped away. "I'll never forget you."

She pulled me back in and gave me a proper hug. "I'll never forget you either. You were a pain in the *'you know where'*. Now get. I got things to do today." She turned back to the sink. I heard a big sniff come from her. A corresponding sniffle tugged at my heart too. She'd become my surrogate mother and hadn't even applied for the position. I vowed to stay in touch with her.

As I left Mrs. Cribbs in the kitchen and made my way down to the barn I realized I would miss the quiet, gentle rhythm of the ranch. I loved being a PI, but there was something about working with your hands and enjoying the benefits brought about by all your hard work. It felt right somehow.

Maybe I'd start a garden in my back yard and grow a few vegetables. I'd wow Polly with my new culinary skills, taught to me by a patient Mrs. Cribbs. Polly would never believe I could make something other than pasta and salad.

The barn was still a few feet away when Caleb came through the open door, stopping when he saw me.

"Hey, Caleb. Thought I'd come see if Shay had her

baby yet."

"No, but she's close."

An awkward pause hung between us. Ever since I'd gotten my memories back Caleb had pulled within himself. And I knew he regretted telling me he'd liked me for so long. The only way I knew how to deal with this situation was head on. He turned to go back into the barn so I hurried forward and grabbed his arm.

"Caleb, wait."

He stopped and looked down at me, the shade from his hat hiding his eyes. It took a few long seconds before he spoke.

"What do you want Dixie?" He cussed. "I mean Shelby."

"I guess I'll always be Dixie to you, won't I?"

A wry smile quirked the corner of his mouth. "Yeah, you'll always be my Dixie." He shifted his stance and hooked his thumbs in the loop of his jeans.

"Caleb. You are one of the nicest men I know."

"I know where this is going. *But you'll always be my friend.*" Bitterness tinged his voice and it hurt my heart. He needed someone in his life, too.

"Yes, you will. You did nothing wrong. I did nothing wrong. There's just never been anyone but Tank for me and even without my memory he was always there. You knew that."

Caleb shrugged and looked over my shoulder into the distance. Finally he gave a droll smile and chucked me under the chin like he did when he asked me to the dance.

"Yeah, I did. But I always hoped." He pushed the brim of his hat back onto his head. The fine lines around his chocolate eyes crinkled when he finally smiled. "Tank said he'd wait for you in the car. I can't leave Shay; she's too close, so I'll say my good-byes here." He leaned in and brushed my lips with his. "See ya... Dixie." He turned and disappeared into the barn.

I stood there for a few seconds, a bit stunned by the sweet kiss, then turned back to the house, my suitcase and Tank.

Sue Barr

Chapter Twenty-One

Well, shoot. That didn't go as planned.

Tank rubbed the back of his neck and paced in the guest bedroom Polly had graciously offered until he and Shelby had a chance to work things out. All the scenarios he'd hashed through in his mind never had him staying at Polly's. He just assumed Shelby would come home, they'd talk about what happened and be right back where they were before the fictitious break-up.

He gave a derisive snort.

That plan hit the garbage before it even saw the light of day. Any dreams he had of her leaping into his arms and begging to be reunited had been stomped into the ground when she opted to stay at their house—alone—while she adjusted and went back to work.

He tried to give her some space, but it was hard. Everything in him screamed to camp outside her door and make sure she was okay. He knew Regis was in jail. He knew there was no further threat from Carlos, but until he held her in his arms and could feel her breathe, he wouldn't rest.

Shelby wasn't making it easy either. Earlier in the week, he asked how things were going. She cut him off, said she was on a case and was too busy to talk. He knew that to be a bold-faced lie. She'd had maybe two phone calls since she'd returned. Three months absent in the PI business is equivalent to eternity and would-be clients found others to do the job.

Yesterday he brought a coffee for her and Polly and while he cooled his heels, in the front lobby no less, Caleb called and she smiled. Actually smiled. Not for him, but Caleb. She smiled for the other guy, who'd called to check up on *his* girl.

He'd seen the exchange between Caleb and Shelby outside the barn and almost jumped him there. He pictured himself punching Caleb's face and felt a grim satisfaction deep in his gut. But that would last maybe four seconds because Caleb was a ninth degree black belt and Tank wouldn't get in another easy hit.

He could shoot him, but then Grizzle, who called himself Raymonde now, would take him out. Grizzle had been the best sniper he ever commanded and stayed in touch with Caleb. Tank, Grizzle, and Caleb, whom they called Cowboy and Dango, the lone Australian working for the LAPD, had been a tight unit within the Special Forces. The four of them were brothers and friends. A bond forged by trust.

Still, friend or not Caleb had to be neutralized and his options were dwindling. He and Shelby were going to have a serious sit down talk and that meant getting her to stay in the same room with him. Alone.

When he realized he'd wear out the carpet, pacing back and forth strategizing, he checked his watch. Shelby would be at the shop in a few minutes and he meant to corner her there and remind her they still had a lot of love between them.

****

Staring into space wasn't helping me get any work done. Not that there was a lot to do. Being away from the job for over three months hurt my business. I had a contact at the courthouse who'd give me bail jumpers when things were slow. If business didn't pick up, I'd give her a call, but not just yet. I couldn't concentrate on anything right now.

My brain refused to stay focused on anything other than how I felt about Tank. Did I love him or was that just a residual memory from before he left me? At the ranch, when I was in his arms I'd felt like that was where I belonged, but since then I'd had to time to calm down and put everything into perspective.

Once again the hurt he let me suffer through, because he didn't trust me to keep his secret, tore at me. Was I willing to let that go and move forward, or was it time to say good-bye for real this time?

Then I'd remember how he looked when he found me at the ranch. I'd never seen such raw emotion on his face before and it made me think maybe he did love me in a way that could last a lifetime.

I was so confused. This wasn't getting me anywhere. There was nothing keeping me at the office, except the distant hope someone would call with a job. A change of scenery was called for and I knew the perfect spot. Polly's daddy had a remote cabin he used for hunting near a lake on their property. Always well stocked I could camp out there for a week or two, sort through my thoughts and make a decision.

Polly sat at her computer, playing Solitaire.

"Don't you ever get tired playing that game?"

She looked up. "Not really. I thought reading a magazine would be too tacky. This way, if anyone did come into the office, at least it looks like I was working on the computer."

The logic made sense and I nodded. "Good to know you've got the company's best interest at heart, Pol."

She watched me pace the floor. Something I'd been doing a lot lately. Soon there'd be a permanent path worn out in front of her desk.

"Are you going to tell me what you're thinking or should we play twenty questions?"

I stopped pacing.

"Is anyone using your daddy's cabin right now?"

"You mean the one at Walker Lake?"

"Yeah, the one you and I used to sneak off to when we skipped class."

"No one has used it for a while. Why?"

I shoved my hands in the front pocket of my jeans. "I need to figure out what's going on between Tank and me. I can't keep him at arm's length much longer. It's not fair to him or me."

Polly brought up my appointment calendar on her computer. "The only thing you have scheduled is your annual physical with Dr. Kaufman. I'll reschedule that for the next week." A few clicks. "There, you're clear."

Before I walked out the door I turned. "Polly?"

"What hon'?"

"Don't tell Tank. If he knew where I was, he'd be all over me like a scratchy wool sweater."

"I don't know..."

"Please. I need time alone."

"I don't like it, but alright. Keep your cell phone charged and call me if you want to talk."

****

A block away, in a rusted out van with Beryl's

Plumbing emblazoned on the side, a man sat huddled with a pair of headsets on. Good thing he'd installed the bug a few years ago, otherwise he'd have no idea how to locate her. Time was of the essence if he was going to get ahead of her.

****

Where the heck was Shelby?

Tank bit back a curse. He'd gone to her office and neither she nor Polly was there. A quick drive by their house turned up negative and her Aunt's Austen-Healy Sprite wasn't in the garage either.

Where was she?

Tank prowled around Polly's house until he found her enjoying a coffee out on the terrace. She sat in an oversized wicker chair on the shaded porch which overlooked her wild and colorful gardens. Rolling hills spread out before the cool, fragrant room. Polly looked up and smiled as he joined her.

"Want some coffee?" She reached for the carafe on the table.

"Sure, thanks." He pulled up a chair and grabbed a croissant out of the basket. "I stopped by the office this morning."

Polly paused, mid sip. Carefully she placed her cup back onto the saucer.

"Really? It's closed."

Tank stirred sugar into the rich, fragrant brew. "I know and I went by Shelby's place."

"She's not home, either."

His patience was wearing thin. "I realized that when I stopped by."

"Do you want anything else?" She gestured toward the plate of muffins.

Tank tilted closer to her chair. Polly sat as still as a mouse hoping the cat wouldn't see her. "I don't need any muffins, and I don't need more coffee. I don't need anything else you might offer in the way of food. What I *need* is Shelby's whereabouts. Mind sharing? I know she wouldn't go anywhere without telling you."

Polly turned and looked him square in the eye. "I promised her this morning at the office I wouldn't tell you where she'd gone. Believe me when I say she's safe and will come back in a week."

Frustrated, Tank sat back in the chair. "I love her, Polly."

"I know."

Polly was silent for a few minutes, her gaze centered on the far corner of her garden, or maybe even beyond it. Tank twisted sideways to see what she was looking at, but after the trimmed hedges surrounding the garden there was nothing but pasture and a dense forest skirting the edges. Deciding Polly wasn't really looking at anything, Tank asked, "What are you thinking about?"

She sipped her coffee and then, smiling slightly into her cup said, "I was debating whether I should sell that little hunting lodge in the forest. Daddy always keeps it well stocked with supplies, but nobody goes there anymore and that's too bad because there's this huge fireplace, just begging to be used. But, it's too isolated. Why, anyone could get into it if they knew the key was under the tin can at the corner of the wood pile."

Polly finished her coffee and stood, glancing at her watch. "Oh my, will you look at the time. I'm going to be late for my manicure appointment. I've got a whole week of pampering scheduled, what with the office closed."

She turned on her heel and as she swayed into the house

she called back over her shoulder, "Take lots of bug spray."

Tank sat staring after her. Bug spray? What was all that nonsense about the cabin? Who cared if it was isolated, with no one around? Why would she tell him where the key was? Wasn't that the object of hiding it, so no one would find it and use the place? His mind clicked a few more times and then the corners of his mouth spread into a huge grin. Thank you, Polly.

He'd name their first daughter after her.

Sue Barr

According to Plan

Chapter Twenty-Two

The first warning should have been the huge log across the road. I stopped the car and got out to assess how heavy it was and if I could move it by myself.

The second warning should have been the convenience of a truck approaching so soon after I'd stopped. But with my mind on the tree, Tank and everything else, it passed by without one little red flag popping up.

I couldn't see the driver as he'd already jumped out of his truck, but he called over, "Hang on. I've got a rope." Grateful for the unexpected help, I turned back to the tree and tried to figure out where the best place would be to winch it to the truck. That was when I noticed the base of the tree wasn't broken, but neatly sawn in two.

Finally the two red flags got my attention, but it was too late. An arm clamped across my shoulders, pinning me against his chest and a foul smelling cloth was thrust in my face. I struggled and then nothing.

****

Tank finished packing and was headed for his motorcycle when his phone dinged indicating a text message. Anxious to get to the cabin he thought about ignoring the persistent dinging, but it was too ingrained in him to make sure it wasn't something vital.

His stomach went into free fall when he read the message from Liz.

Regis has posted bail and had been released that morning. Surveillance showed he spent some time in a plumbing van, but after that the agent lost him. When they located the van they discovered recording devices and realized he had a bug in Shelby's office.

His stomach cramped at the thought of Regis knowing Shelby would be at the cabin, alone. Tank dropped his duffel bag on the manicured lawn and raced for his motorcycle, praying he'd get to the cabin before Regis. No way would he lose her a second time to him.

He gunned the engine and gravel sprayed everywhere as he tore down the drive and sped off for the only road leading in to Walker Lake. As he came around a corner, a dirty white truck almost side swiped him before correcting its course and continuing on.

"Idiot," Tank muttered. He leaned into the next corner, took the left fork and then the next right turn onto a slightly overgrown road leading to the cabin. He'd gone maybe two miles when the sight before him stopped his breath.

Aunt Tillie's vintage car sat parked in front of a downed tree. There was no one sign of Shelby. He parked the bike and ran to the car. Shelby's purse lay on the front seat, her keys in the ignition.

He touched the hood of the car. Still warm. He looked around. There was no indication she'd gone into the woods and it was eerily silent. It didn't take long to see where the tree had been cut and in the sandy soil it was obvious some kind of struggle had occurred, as footprints were clearly visible.

The truck! The one he passed on the highway. It had to be Regis, headed back into town. Regis couldn't go to his home, so where would he take Shelby? And was she still alive?

****

The thought of turning my head had bile flooding my mouth. I swallowed it back because some kind of tape covered my mouth and my hands were tied behind my back. I'd choke to death if I didn't get a handle on the fear.

The memory of being attacked by the stranger near the cut tree and the foul smelling cloth rushed back. Carefully I assessed the situation. By the look of the room I was on a bed in a cheap motel room.

The guy hadn't tied my legs. Which was good, but he'd removed my shoes and stripped off my pants. Relief flooded me. At least he hadn't raped me. Yet. If I had to run, I didn't care if I was only in my panties. My father had drummed into me that modesty had no place in my vocabulary when it came to survival.

Pushing through the nausea, I tried to sit. It was at that moment I heard the card lock on the door activating. Falling back on the bed, I pretended I was still out cold.

My attacker had his back to me and he dragged a suitcase in behind him. His build was familiar and I closed my eyes again when he started to turn, but I'd caught a glimpse and it was enough for me to know his identity.

Regis.

When did he get out of jail, and what was he planning? He moved around the room and I risked opening one eye just a sliver. He'd thrown the suitcase on a table and opening it, brought out duct tape and rope and laid them beside the suitcase. My heart rate tripled when he rummaged in a plastic grocery bag and brought out a tin of lighter fluid.

Now what? I could probably roll off the bed, but I had

no way to open the door with my hands tied behind my back.

Without turning, Regis said, "You have awakened. Excellent."

How'd he know? Like he could read my mind he said, "Your accelerated rate of breathing alerted me to your conscious state."

He faced me and frowned. I shrank into the mattress when he approached the bed.

"No, no, no. That will not do. I need you to be like this." He pulled me up by my armpits until I sat propped upright against the pillows. I tensed, ready to kick him the first chance I had.

He anticipated and said, "Do not do anything ill conceived, or I will be forced to confine you to the bed."

If I was tied to the bed, I couldn't run. I hated him and hated this situation, but for now, all I could do was glare while he fussed with my hair. Satisfied everything was placed how he wanted, he trailed one thin finger down my cheek and I flinched when he went so far as to caress the outside of my breast.

I twisted away at the touch. He hauled me back into a sitting position.

"Do not make me hurt you," he admonished in his whiny, nasal voice. "I do not *want* to hurt you. I love you. All I have ever wanted was to touch you. You never let me touch you like you let *him*."

And you never will, you sicko. I wished I could telepathically tell this pathetic piece of garbage how much I loathed him. The bed dipped when he sat beside me, his hip touching mine. He skimmed his hand across my belly, moving upward and I sucked air in through my nose when he cupped my breast through the tee shirt and bra.

"This will not do. I need to feel your skin."

He slid off the bed, rummaged through his suitcase again and with a flourish, brought out a huge carving knife.

A sick smile twisted his face as he came back toward the bed. "This will do the job. Please do not move. I would not want to accidentally mar your beautiful skin while I remove your articles of clothing."

I began to hyperventilate and couldn't drag in enough air through my nostrils. My clothing had become the least of my worries. Why would he be carrying around such a huge knife? Regis approached the bed and craziness shone through his beady little eyes. Why hadn't I told Tank I loved him? I didn't want to die with that being my last thought.

****

As he tore up the highway in the same direction he'd seen the truck traveling, Tank looked down every side road and checked parking lots of diners, hotels, and motels. The longer it took to find them, the harder it would become. Sunset was only an hour off and then, in the dark, it'd be like finding a needle in the proverbial haystack.

He could put out an APB, but he all he had was a vague description of an older model, white truck with one headlight missing. Screeching to a halt, he swerved around and sped into the parking lot of the Lazy Daze Motel.

The very last parking spot, beside a minivan, held a truck that looked a lot like the one he'd passed. Tank hid his bike behind the motel's dumpster and approached the door directly opposite the parked vehicle. The lights were on in the room, but everything was silent, not even the background noise of a television filtered out. There was no way of knowing if Regis was in there with Shelby, although this was the most logical room for them to be. No one would see him drag a person in, as it was at the end of a long row of rooms.

He stopped. A man's voice could be heard talking in the room. Sounded like Regis. He hesitated until he heard a loud thump and the man screamed. "I said do not move! You did not have my permission to move!"

Tank didn't wait another second. With a well-placed kick, the door blew open and in one sweeping glance he saw Shelby rolling off the bed onto the floor, her mouth taped and hands tied behind her back. When Regis swiveled toward the door, Tank saw the carving knife in his hand.

Time slowed as Tank feinted left, then rolled right, reaching for the gun tucked in the back waistband of his jeans. As Regis moved to his right, falling for Tank's fake out, Tank pulled out the gun and squeezed the trigger.

Regis halted and the knife clattered to the floor. His expression registered surprise as he looked down at his chest. At first there was nothing but a tiny hole, then a dark red stain spread across his sweater vest. It only took seconds, but he looked back at Tank, sank to his knees and crumpled to the ground.

Tank kept the gun trained on Regis while he kicked the knife away from the now lifeless hand. When he was sure Regis was dead, he rushed to Shelby who was still trying to kick away from Regis. Her tee shirt was cut down the middle and one bra strap had been sliced through.

Tank picked her up, sat on the bed with her in his lap and cradled her.

"I couldn't lose you again." He said, rocking them both. He wouldn't let go, ever. If he had his way, she'd never be out of his sight again.

Shelby wiggled until he looked down at her. Big blue eyes stared up at him, over the industrial green tape covering her mouth.

"I forgot about the duct tape. I'm sorry, sweetheart." He

peeled back the tape, wincing with her as bits of skin came off with it. "Oh baby. I'm so sorry."

"My hands," Shelby croaked.

****

Hours later, after police and EMS had cleared us, Tank and I watched the ambulance drive away with the body of Regis. Even with a warm woolen blanket covering me, I couldn't stop the shivers rippling through my body. That would have been me if Tank hadn't arrived when he did. Tank must have seen me shaking, because he drew me against his chest and rubbed my back with long, soothing strokes until the shivers abated.

I turned into his shoulder and tears pricked the back of my eyes. Too much had happened. My coping mechanism was shutting down. How many shocks can a body take anyway? I'd almost been kidnapped by Big Boss. Regis tried to blow my head off and then the sick pervert chloroformed me and who knew what he'd have done if Tank had been even one minute later. Visions of the lighter fluid had my imagination racing.

"Take me home." I mumbled into his chest.

"Polly's offered to drive you back to her place."

Polly had arrived shortly after the police. We all agreed I shouldn't be alone tonight, as I couldn't stop shaking and was continually on the verge of tears. But, when I realized I could have died and hadn't told Tank I loved him, I needed to be with only him.

"No. Just you and me."

Tank pulled me in tighter. "Back to our place?"

I nodded my head, burrowing deeper into his chest. If I could crawl inside his skin, I would. I needed to be close to him.

"Anything you want darlin', I'd give you the moon if you asked."

If I squeezed any harder, I'd crack his ribs.

*****

The grandfather clock in the hall chimed midnight when we finally stepped through the front door of our house. Polly insisted Tank use her car and fluttered big green eyes at a cute young trooper who jumped at the chance to drive her home.

It was surreal. My purse, keys, and car were back on the road to the lake and Tank's bike was at the motel. But all that didn't matter. We were alive and at our bedroom door. Now would be a good time to tell Tank I loved him.

Resolved to speak the words no matter what, I turned and froze. His face grim, he stalked toward me. Recognizing that dangerous glint in his eyes, I backed into the bedroom.

"Do you—?" I gulped, "Do you think this is a good idea?"

"This is the best idea I've had in months."

"What exactly do you think you're doing?" I demanded, noting that I sounded excited and breathy. No small wonder. If he didn't tear my borrowed clothes off, I'd to do it for him.

"I almost lost you."

"But, you didn't. I'm here, and I'm safe."

"Shelby, if I don't make love to you, right here, right now, I'll go out of my mind." He stopped inches from me. "I can't be gentle. I need you too bad to be nice."

I needed him as much as he needed me, if not more, so I reached up and pulled him down to kiss me.

*****

After what seemed like hours we cuddled beneath the duvet.

"Are you okay?" His voice was hoarse in my ear.

"Yes, but I don't think I could handle that again."

He chuckled and pinned me against his chest when I would have rolled away.

"You know I never would have left if I didn't think it was the right thing to do?"

A small part of me knew what he said was true, but I couldn't let go of the fact he hadn't trusted me with his secret. Down the road, if something else with his job threatened us, would he leave again? How could I know that he was in this marriage all the way?

"Tank, what if—"

He placed his index finger across my lips.

"No what ifs. You never have to worry ever again. Nothing and nobody will take me away from you. Ever."

He propped up on his elbow and gazed down at me. With tender fingers he brushed the hair off my forehead and kissed the scar above my eyebrow. Firm lips moved down the side of my face and paused near the pulse beating at the base of my neck.

"We've done hard and fast. How about soft and slow?" Desire thickened his voice.

My heart swelled with love at the memory of that disastrous game of pool.

"I love you, Tank"

He deepened the kiss and when he pulled away to explore other areas in need of his attention, I heard him whisper, "Love you too. Always have."

Sue Barr

According to Plan

Chapter Twenty-Three

I stared at the slim white wand in my hand.

Blue. All of them were blue. I looked around at the carnage of open boxes on the floor of my bathroom. Every little stick had shown the tiny blue stripe. It was supposed to be pink or red—any color but blue!

Maybe they were defective and I should go across town, go out of state and buy another one to make sure. Tears welled in my eyes. Who was I kidding? They'd all be blue.

I was pregnant.

This was not supposed to happen. At least not right now. We were supposed to enjoy wedded bliss for at least two point five years before having a baby. This had been meticulously planned by me since I was eight years old.

I kept my scheduled appointment with Doctor Kaufmann and he confirmed my suspicions. I was about four months along. Here I thought it was Mrs. Cribbs cooking that had me gaining weight. All that time I was pregnant and hadn't known it.

I heard keys hitting the hall table and flew down the hallway, launched myself into Tank's arms and rained kisses all over his gorgeous face.

"I'm so glad you're home." I grabbed his hand and tugged him down to the kitchen. "Are you hungry? Dinner's almost ready." I babbled because I was nervous and didn't know how to tell him about the baby. Tank allowed himself to be dragged along, stopping just inside the kitchen door.

"I think I'd like some dessert now." He tugged me back into his arms and slanting his lips over mine, kissed me hungrily.

He walked us up against the wall and palm to palm our hands mated. With a sweet slowness he stretched our hands above my head. His whole body pressed against mine and I rubbed along the length of him, like a cat. Unhurried, he blazed a trail down the outside of my arm with his hand, then snaked his arm around my waist. His other hand brushed the top of my shirt. With deceptive languor, he popped open the first button to my blouse. He'd deepened the kiss and had moved on to the second button when the doorbell chimed.

"I'll tell 'em to get lost." Tank lowered his forehead onto mine and with a hard kiss, released me. He raked a hand through his hair and adjusted his jeans before stalking down the hall to the front door. I pressed my hands against my flushed cheeks and took the opportunity to straighten my clothes.

Poor Tank, it was little girls, selling cookies. Girlish giggles followed by his deep voice echoed down the hall. He was toast. He couldn't say no to sweet smiles and childish enthusiasm. And I'm sure the mother's escorting them enjoyed the eye candy at the door. I knew I would.

When he came returned to the kitchen with four boxes, I arched an eyebrow. "Four?"

He shrugged and stuffed them into the pantry, then turned and prowled toward me. I recognized the glint in his eye and felt a delicious shudder go through me. Tank scooped me into his arms and holding me close to his chest, bounded up the stairs two at a time.

"Dinner can wait." He growled as he shouldered open

the door to our bedroom and practically threw me onto the bed. He kept his eyes trained on me while he tore his shirt over his head, kicked off his boots and shrugged out of his jeans.

My mouth went dry and I couldn't have said word, even if I wanted. Baby news would have to wait.

****

The next morning I watched Tank eating his breakfast. It was now or never. I had to tell him before my ever expanding belly gave it away.

"Tank, would you come with me to get some things for the house?" I bit into dry toast.

"Sure, what kind of things?' He poured ketchup on his semi-hard eggs. My stomach rolled. At this rate even the toast wouldn't stay down. I sipped my tepid tea.

"Just a few things for the spare room, nothing much." Maybe if I didn't watch him dip his toast into the slimy yolk which had mixed with the thick ketchup... Excusing myself I ran for the bathroom upstairs. A few minutes later I brushed my teeth and went back down to resume eating the dry, cold toast.

After breakfast we went to a large furniture store, although I thought we'd never leave the house. Tank disappeared into our bedroom, only re-appearing when I threatened to come upstairs and drag him down.

He held my hand and snatched kisses whenever he thought no one in the store was looking, not paying too much attention to where we were. His steps faltered when I paused in the little area with children's furniture. He further slowed down when I stopped at a beautiful hand carved rocker, sat in it and began rocking gently.

"Shelby, why are we here?"

I rocked a little harder and couldn't look at him. All I saw were two big feet, planted directly in front of me.

"Shelby." His tone had an edge to it.

I stopped rocking. Running my fingers on the arm of the rocker I asked. "What color would you like to paint the room if it's a boy?" I dared to peep up.

I had never seen Tank at a loss for words. I probably never would again. He was so still I wasn't sure he heard me. His face was devoid of emotion, so I repeated, "Tank, what color...?"

"I heard you." He pulled me out of the rocker and lifted me into his arms. His heart thundered in his chest. I didn't know if he was happy, mad, or indifferent and I stumbled back when he released me and let out an ear-splitting whoop before pulling me back in his arms.

Patrons jumped and store clerks came to see what all the fuss was. They arrived in time to see me crushed in a tight bear hug again, while Tank twirled around, kissing me over and over.

Laughing, I pushed on his shoulders. "Tank, the child will come out dizzy if you don't put me down."

"Are you all right?" He almost dropped me in his haste to set me on terra firma, placing the palm of his hand on my little rounded belly. The tiny bulge alone should have told me I was pregnant.

"I'm going to have a baby. Women have been doing this for millennia." I loved the feel of his big hand resting on my belly, on our child.

"I know, but this is my first time, so cut me some slack." He hugged me again.

"Uh, Tank. We're in public." My voice was muffled as I spoke into his chest.

"I don't care." But he did loosen his arms and allow me

to breath. Snagging my hand in his large one, he dragged me through the store, not stopping until we were in our new jeep. He half turned in his seat.

"When?" No beating around the bush with Tank.

"About four months." I could see the wheels turning in Tank's mind, calculating.

"You were pregnant before the explosion." He shook his head in disbelief. "We only made love once."

"That's all it takes."

Tank reached across the gearshift, pulled me close and kissed me again. The kiss was sweet, yet demanding at the same time. He caressed my cheek and whispered, "You can't know how excited I am."

Then he decided we needed things for the baby and me. We bought vitamins, every book he could find on pregnancy and childcare, stopping only when I refused to buy a jogging stroller. Totally exhausted when we arrived home I wanted to lie down. I also needed to pee, again, and made my way to our bedroom upstairs. Although the room lay in darkness, I didn't need a light to find the bathroom.

When I came out of the ensuite, I stopped at the sight of what lay before me. The room was filled with votive candles and crimson rose petals were sprinkled over the duvet. A glass of milk sat in a bucket full of ice, the previously chilled champagne placed on the floor beside the bed and Tank waited—a small black box in his hand.

So this was why he took so long to get ready this morning. I approached and took the box he held out. After a quick, questioning glance, I raised the lid.

Nestled in the velvet was a square cut diamond set in platinum gold, with two gleaming emeralds on either side. My heart hammered and I could barely choke out words.

"You found them?"

"Had to crawl through the shrubbery by the front porch, but yeah, I found them."

"I always regretted throwing my rings at you." With wondering eyes, I looked about the room. Never in my wildest dreams, and I'd had a few, would I have expected this. "Why all the romance? We're already married."

"I planned on taking you out for a romantic dinner and when we came home, I'd carry you here, have a champagne toast and do this proper. Our whole married life was built on a foundation of lies. But now we've got a clean slate."

He took the box out of my shaking hand and bent down on one knee. My breath stuttered as he slid the familiar ring on my fourth finger.

Holding my hand, he looked up at me. "I think I loved you before I met you. You make me weak in the knees, every day. These past few months have been hell and I don't want to waste another moment. I want to fight with you. Laugh and love with you..." He placed a big hand on my belly, "...have children with you. Shelby Marie Stewart-Steele, will you marry me, again?"

Tears slipped down my cheeks and I dropped to my knees. I held his face in my hands, and looked first into his green and then blue eye. "Yes. I'll marry you, Jackson Montgomery Steele."

Hours later, snuggled close against his chest, I grinned into the dark and thought about the only other thing which could render him speechless. I almost shook him awake, but decided I'd tell him in the morning, just as he was about to take a big gulp of coffee.

I slid into sleep… *Hope he's ready for twins.*

THE END

If you enjoyed this book, please help other readers discover it by leaving a review on the retail site of your choice, and/or Goodreads.

About the Author:

Bestselling author, Sue Barr, resides in beautiful Southwestern Ontario, Canada with her retired air force husband, close to their sons and families. She's also in servitude to her cats and has been knows to rescue a kitten or two, or three...in an attempt to keep her cat-lady-in-training status current, although she has deviated from the appointed path and rescued a few dogs as well.

When not busy writing, Sue loves to spend time with family and friends. She sings along with the radio in the car, hoping no one sees, has been known to laugh until it hurts, sneaks a few non-healthy things.... *okay*.... a LOT of non-healthy things into her diet, and thanks God daily for allowing her to have this wonderful life.

www.suebarrauthor.com

I can do all things through Christ who strengthens me.
Philippians 4:13